Also by Martin Stevenson

*Once Upon a Time in the Waste:
Tales of Utter Filth*

*Twice Upon a Time in the Waste:
Twice the Filth*

The Reincarnation Bureau

Once Upon a Time in the Waste

Lockdown and Beyond

Martin Stevenson

Copyright © Martin Stevenson, 2024

The moral right of Martin Stevenson to be identified as the author of this work has been asserted in accordance with the Copyright, Designs and Patents Act, 1988.
All rights reserved. No part of this publication may be reproduced or transmitted in any form or by any means, electronic or mechanical, including photocopy, recording, or any information storage and retrieval system, without permission in writing from the publisher.
This is a work of fiction. The names, characters, businesses, organisations, places and events and incidents portrayed in it are either the product of the author's imagination or are used fictitiously. Any resemblance to actual persons, living or dead, events or localities, is entirely coincidental.

ISBN 979-8-8769-3821-3

Four Bears Publishing

Cover art by Jenny Langridge for which I am thrice grateful.

To anyone who has suffered or is still suffering because of Covid 19

Introduction

So here we are again, at least those of us who survived the pandemic. My heartfelt condolences to anyone who lost family or friends through the Covid nightmare. The rest of us stoically continue to stand by our bins and hope that we are making a difference. From the bin where *I* stand, that is not very clear. Despite all our individual and organised recycling endeavours, the forces of darkness and decay are at large and working to subvert our efforts. Here are a few examples.

I have learned that criminal gangs are creating enormous illegal dumps, not only in the UK but worldwide. Shockingly, many of them are located at or near beauty spots and there are an estimated one thousand new illegal dump sites appearing every year.

Pollution is now even affecting our planet's geology. At the time of writing, a new type of sedimentary rock has been found in eleven countries across five continents. These rocks form when molten plastic cools and merges with rock to form a plastic/rock fusion. Such rocks have been named plastistones.

And in the Atacama Desert, an enormous discoloured area has been spotted from space that turns out to be worn clothing from the fast fashion industry. I'll say that again. The mountain of clothing is so big it can be seen from space!

So, what can we learn from all this? Clearly, fly-tipping at scale has become more lucrative than the illegal drugs trade for criminal gangs. And why wouldn't they do it when the comparative penalties if they get caught are minor?

At least people in glasshouses can now throw plastistones.

And if you are ever feeling a bit of a chill while crossing the Atacama Desert, no problem; that mountain in front of you is likely made of jumpers.

We continue to find new ways of messing up our world and you may wonder if we are beyond redemption.

Well, I can tell you it's not all doom and gloom. People are fighting back. In Sweden for example, the bins have been designed to give personal encouragement, as you will discover. I did not make this up!

And if your own bins are not so supportive, then fear not. There is a last line of defence. Enter Albert, Clive and the crew of Dedbury recycle centre.

Reviews

"So many throw-away lines!" Recycling Weekly

"Has this author reached his fly-tipping point?" Trash Today

"The War and Peace of recycling. Without the war …
or the peace … or much recycling." Anon

Dump Fever

I must go down to the dump again
To the filthy dump and the trash
And all I ask is a tall skip and I'll sort my life in a flash
With my binbags, some old rags and beer bottles clinking
Join the long queues with some old shoes
And some wishful thinking

Episodes

Roll Model
Albie
Sgt. Pill Popper's Lonely Hearts
Identity Crisis
Purple Urkle
Reality Check
Undue Influence
The Dedbury Falcon
Managing Expectations
More Lies, More Damned Lies and not much Recycling
Garbo
Message from a Bottle

Extras

Bonus Stories

Infestation
Fairies: Assemble
Fairies: Endgame
Old Friends

The Third Clive Dumper Songbook
Clive's poetry and thoughts

Roll Model

"Toilet Rolls!" declared Clive through his facemask. He was sitting on the bench opposite the recycle centre.

Albert, sitting next to him at the opposite end of the bench, but at the required social distance, attempted to shuffle away from him but was unable to do so without falling off it.

"I am not in the habit of carrying toilet rolls with me, at least not yet. If you have a pressing personal need to attend to then the toilet is just across the road."

"No. I mean, I have discovered why there is a shortage of toilet rolls."

"I thought that was obvious. Panic buying."

Clive shook his head, sagely. "You would think so but it turns out that's not the whole story. And by the way, I hate panic buyers."

Albert pulled his own facemask aside to bite into his sandwich then pulled a face.

"What's wrong?"

"All I had left in my cupboard was cheese slices. It's not the same as real cheese."

Clive was sympathetic. "I feel for you brother." He examined the contents of his own sandwich. "This is Wensleydale. Too crumbly, but what can you do?"

"Do you think we'll ever see any of our normal cheese again, what with all this panic buying going on?"

Clive bit into his sandwich again and he also pulled a face.

"I truly hope so. How can life go on without proper Cheddar? All those panic buyers should be locked up. I have a song about them. I call it "Panic Buyer's Lament". Do you want to hear it?"

"Why am I not surprised?" sighed Albert. "Do I have a choice?"

"Well, I'm going to sing it. I need to get it off my chest. It's up to you if you listen or not."

"But I'm sitting right next …"

Albert did not have chance to finish his sentence because Clive had begun.

Non panic buyer

You've got sixteen going on seventeen
Toilet rolls, I have none
I'm almost beat, I'm down to one sheet
And soon that will be gone

You have sixteen going on seventeen
Toilet rolls in your hand
Andrex or Tescos, that's how the mess goes
You do not care which brand.

Totally too prepared are you
To face a world of mess
You have so many, I haven't any
You simply couldn't care less

You have sixteen going on seventeen
Loo rolls in every room
You've all the paper, I just have vapour
And that will run out soon

Panic buyer

I have sixteen going on seventeen
Guess what I'm sitting on
My bum is happy, yours will be crappy
The conclusion is foregone

I have sixteen going on seventeen
You haven't really tried
Go help yourself, go clear out a shelf
Happy to be your guide

Totally unprepared are you
And my advice is clear
I'm panic buying, you're hardly trying
While the pandemic draws near

Please no scoffing, now I'm coughing
And I'm in quarantine
I took a six pack then grabbed a twelve pack
Covered in Covid 19

"Anyway," said Albert as soon as Clive finished, "you were saying something about toilet rolls."

Clive now had a satisfied smile on his face as if the act of performing the song had lifted a load from his shoulders. "Yes. Toilet rolls. It seems that there are two separate markets for toilet rolls. The domestic market and the business market. Suppliers to the domestic market make them all soft and cushiony in pretty, plastic packages. These are for the general public who, we might suppose, all have sensitive little botties."

"Sensitive big botties, some of them," added Albert.

Clive was annoyed with Albert for interrupting his flow and threw him a stern look. "Yes. Sensitive little ones and big ones. And this country has a lot of them."

"Everyone I know has one," interrupted Albert again.

Clive raised his voice to show his disapproval. "As I was saying, on the other hand, the toilet rolls for businesses ... I'm talking like offices, shopping centres, airports etc. are poorer quality and are often served up on huge rolls. When people are working, they are doing their doo-doo at work. But now they are all at home, and so using a lot more rolls at home than they used to, especially if they are watching the news a lot. The manufacturers of the business type of rolls would need to retool if they were to switch to the domestic market and they are not willing to do so because of the cost and the supposed temporary nature of the crisis."

"Wow," said Albert. "You really have been studying the toilet roll situation. Is this your new hobby or are you thinking of becoming a professional toilet rollologist?"

"Maybe that would be better than being a trashologist, which is what we both are right now." He pointed to the stream of rubbish-laden cars lined up to get into the recycle centre.

"Look at them all. It's unbelievable. We have never had queues as long as these. All these people are now at home. It is a chance for them to be doing something really creative. They could be taking up new hobbies. They could be learning a new language, learning to play an instrument, take up painting. But what do they all do? They decide to clear out their attics or other rooms in their house that haven't seen the light of day for possibly decades. And then they bring it all here."

Some of the drivers in the queue were evidently becoming frustrated by the wait and honked at each other.

Albert nodded in agreement. "Even people who already have hobbies are suffering."

"What do you mean?"

"I was watching the news and they were talking about the nudists in Czechoslovakia."

"Nudists!" exclaimed Clive, "Being a nudist is not a hobby. It's more like just being antisocial. Why are *they* suffering?"

"Apparently they are still allowed to go out and do the nude thing they do, but their government says they all have to wear a particular item of clothing and they don't like it."

"I can see why a nudist might object to that. What is it they are all being forced to wear?"

"Face masks."

Clive rolled his eyes but Albert was keen to mention another thing that was preying on his mind.

"I had an idea about another way the virus is spreading. Money."

"Money?"

"Yes, money. People touch their cash and pass it around. You're bound to pick up something dodgy if you do that all the time."

Clive nodded in agreement. "I can see that, but what do you do about it? Put it in the dishwasher!" He laughed.

"I was thinking about it until I heard about some guy in South Korea. He was worried about the same thing so he put all his savings in the microwave to kill all the bugs."

"And did it work?"

"Yes. But all his money got burnt. He took what was left of it back to his bank but they refused to accept it."

"That only goes to confirm my original suspicions about this crisis."

Albert looked puzzled. "What do you mean?"

"Right from the start I said it won't be the virus that wipes us all out."

"What will it be then?"

"Stupidity." He looked up at the sound of what could be the beginning of a riot coming from inside the recycle centre. "And speaking of stupidity, come on, we'd better go see if we can calm the situation down over there."

* * *

As they walked briskly back into the centre, Albert could not help noticing the frustration on the faces of driver after driver even though most of them were wearing masks inside their cars. He smiled at each one as he passed by until he came to a driver who happened to be a woman. He did a double-take when he saw she was not wearing a mask but a full-sized Buzz Lightyear helmet. He stopped to stare. The woman turned to face him, rolled down her window and pressed a button on the side of her helmet. "To infinity and beyond!" barked the helmet.

He had to run to catch up with Clive. "Did you see that?"

Clive did not stop. "See what?"

"Buzz Lightyear is here doing recycling."

"This crisis has sent you even more doolally than you already were," said Clive.

Even before Albert and Clive reached the general waste, they could hear that some sort of argument was taking place. They had not expected the scene before them. Jabby and Ted were both wielding long handled broomsticks which they were using to pin a large man in an equally large tracksuit to the side of the metal waste skip. He was shouting at a small man who had his back against the general waste skip opposite and cowering fearfully.

"What appears to be the problem?" asked Albert politely.

The big man pointed an accusatory finger at the small man. "Mr Fartypants there bent over the skip and farted at me. Directly at me."

Albert looked at Clive for enlightenment but he just shrugged. He looked back at Mr Big. "I'm not sure I heard you right. Could you say that again?"

"He farted at me. Deliberately. He's trying to kill me. Someone should call the police."

"You think you can be farted to death? I think I am going to need more details before I call the police with this."

Mr Big explained that an Australian doctor was answering viewer's virus queries on TV. One viewer had asked if you could catch the virus from farts and the doctor confirmed that it was possible."

Albert accepted this explanation without question and turned to a nervous looking Mr Fartypants. With a straight face, he asked, "Is this true? Did you fart at this man?"

Mr Fartypants confirmed with a slight nod of his head that he had done so. "But I didn't do it on purpose. It was an involuntary reaction to my bending over the side of the skip."

After this exchange, Albert was unsure how to proceed. He whispered to Clive. "What do you think? Do we call the police?"

"Absolutely not," whispered back Clive. "What we have here is a case of what I was talking about earlier."

"What's that?"

"Stupidity. Let me deal with this."

He addressed Mr Big. "Sir, do you agree that if someone wears a mask over their face, then that would protect us from coughs and sneezes which might pass the virus?"

Mr Big nodded.

"Alright then. So logically it follows that as long as someone wears a mask over their bottom then that would protect us from any virusey air emanating from that area."

"What do you mean, mask on his bottom?" asked Mr Big.

Clive explained. "In place of a mask, in this case I am referring to trousers." He turned and pointed to Fartypants. "Now tell me. Is he wearing trousers?"

Mr Big nodded again.

"I suspect this gentleman is actually wearing two masks. His trousers of course and additionally, one might hope that he is also wearing underpants." He looked to Mr Fartypants, who confirmed with a nod that he was indeed wearing underpants.

"So, he is wearing double protection. My advice to you sir, is to avoid approaching anybody not wearing pants and that way you should stay safe."

With this information, Mr Big visibly relaxed and went back to his car. However, the holdup was frustrating the other waiting drivers even more. Clive decided that he should try to diffuse the tension. He stood on an old pair of step ladders to gain height from which to address the customers. They wound down their windows to hear what he was saying.

"We apologise for the delay ladies and gentlemen. Please be patient. We don't want to make this crisis worse than it already is. To help relieve your boredom, I will sing a song for you and you are all welcome to join in. The song is called Corona Quarantine. When you hear the chorus, you will get the idea.

Everybody stopped what they were doing to listen to Clive.

Corona Quarantine

In our house, where we are bored
We have Netflix, praise the Lord
We stay in, don't go for strolls
We all want to guard, our toilet rolls

We check our phones, we sit and Tweet
Social media, is how we meet
We shop online, we drink caffeine
We are waiting for, a new vaccine

We all live in Corona quarantine
Corona quarantine, Corona quarantine
We all live in Corona quarantine
Corona quarantine, Corona quarantine

We wash our hands, clean everything
While we are social, distancing
Let us all begin to sing

We all live in Corona quarantine
Corona quarantine, Corona quarantine
We all live in Corona quarantine
Corona quarantine, Corona quarantine

We wear our masks, don't cough or sneeze
We don't want to cause, anxieties
We may be sick, or in distress
But we want to thank, the NHS

We all live in Corona quarantine
Corona quarantine, Corona quarantine
We all live in Corona quarantine
Corona quarantine, Corona quarantine
We all live in Corona quarantine
Corona quarantine, Corona quarantine
We all live in Corona quarantine
Corona quarantine, Corona quarantine

When he finished, Ms Hunter came up from her office to thank Clive for diffusing the situation.

"It worked this time," said Clive, "but what about tomorrow and the next day?"

"Luckily there is no tomorrow," she replied.

Albert looked alarmed. "What? No tomorrow? Is the virus that bad?"

"In a way," she said. "I have just heard from head office that the recycle centre will be closed until it is safe to come back to work. Today is our last day. So that's why there's no tomorrow."

She looked around at the waiting drivers. Customers were still singing the chorus after Clive finished. The cars began to move forward again and gradually, the skips began to fill up.

"Yes," she smiled, "the atmosphere around here has completely changed. Well done. Actually, talking about a change of atmosphere, I heard that because so many people were staying at home, pollution in the atmosphere is at an all-time low. If we are all at home then at least we will be able to breathe some fresh air for a change."

"And I thought the air quality had improved because Mr Fartypants just left!" chuckled Clive.

"I'm not so sure about that," said Albert. "I think I know why Mr Fartypants had the problem in the first place."

Ms Hunter looked puzzled. "Why?"

"I was searching for good news amongst all the doom and gloom and like you I heard that because everybody was staying home, there is now hardly any pollution in the atmosphere. I was quite pleased when I heard that, but then I learned that in the first week of panic buying, Tesco sold sixty million tins of baked beans …"

Albie

Albert and Clive sat in silence eating their lunch on the bench opposite the recycle centre. That is to say Clive was eating his lunch. Albert simply sat there, staring into the distance.

Clive finished his cheese sandwich and pulled a copy of Recycling Monthly from his reusable bag.

"Albert, you have a face like a crushed tin can and if you are not going to talk to me, I am going to read aloud from this magazine."

Clearly something was bothering Albert. Clive flicked through the mag to find some interesting story that might cheer him up.

"For the last time, are you going to tell me what's wrong? Because if not, I am going to annoy you by reading from this." He waved the Recycling mag in front of Albert's face to get his attention.

"I don't want to talk about it," said Albert, still staring into the distance.

"So, you can talk then?" No response.

"In that case, you asked for it." Clive rifled through the mag till he found an article that might bring Albert out of his gloom.

"Ah, here's a story about Swedish rubbish bins. This should cheer you up."

In its latest effort to clean up the streets, the Swedish city of Malmö is taking dirty talk to a whole new level.

By installing talking garbage bins that dish out racy audio messages after being fed trash, authorities are hoping for an increase in rubbish being deposited.

Pedestrians that drop trash into one of two bins on one of the city's bridges are rewarded with extremely positive feedback from a sultry, female voice, who offers a range of responses like...

Clive did his best to imitate a sexy female voice.

"Oh, right there, yes!", "Come back soon and do that again!" and "Mmm, a bit more to the left next time."

Loquacious litter bins are not new in Sweden. During the pandemic, the talking bins thanked depositors for adhering to social distancing regulations, but the city council believes that a new era calls for new methods.

A spokesperson said, "The sentences are part of the campaign's intention to get more people to talk about the dirtiest thing there is: littering."

Clive looked across to Albert. No response.

"There are more sentences. Listen to these." He put his sexy voice on again.

"Ooh, yeah, right there."

"Ahh, that was sooo good."

"Hmm, more."

"Push it in deep so I can feel it."

Finally, Albert turned to Clive saying, "You're not helping."

"Then tell me what's bothering you."

Albert really did not wish to discuss it. He attempted a deflection.

"I'm bothered about the number of people who come here every single day and dump stuff that's perfectly good. Every day they bring it in and a lot of it is almost new … or even actually new. They get something new. They get bored with it. Then they come here and they chuck it out. It's all just discarded and ditched."

"And how does that make you feel?"

"It makes me want to scream and shout."

"Then why don't you?"

Albert ignored the question and fell back into the arms of his despair.

Clive gave Albert one of his longest, hardest stares.

"No, I'm not buying it. That's not what's bothering you. If you were at all worried about the kind of stuff that ends up here, you would have mentioned it years ago."

He lowered his voice and added a tinge of concern. "So, tell me. You know you might feel better if you get it off your chest."

Albert turned to him with sad eyes.

"It's about me and Victoria. I have come to realise I know nothing about women. Maybe less than nothing."

"Less than that, probably," added Clive.

Albert did not react. "If you must know, it's Victoria. She's left me."

"Ah, now I understand. When you talked about people dumping stuff that's perfectly good, you were really talking about Victoria dumping you! It's not rubbish being chucked out that bothers you, this is all about you being chucked out."

Clive paused for a moment then asked the obvious question." So, what did you do to bring this about?"

"Me? I did nothing. She found someone else."

Clive shook his head. "I don't believe it. Who?"

"I don't know him. But he has a job at the local sewage works."

"What? She left you for someone with a dirtier and smellier job than yours?"

"Apparently. She's having an affair with him. I'm sure of it. And she never did have a great sense of smell, that's true."

Clive somehow resisted the urge to laugh. He stroked his chin, considering.

"No. I still don't believe it. Tell me how you found out about this. Maybe you're misreading the situation."

"She told me herself."

Clive stroked his chin with more vigour, as if it were an Aladdin's lamp that would bring forth a simple explanation.

"Alright, then tell me what she said. Her exact words."

"She said, I can't see you tonight Albie because I have to see Frank."

"Wait. Albie? She calls you Albie?"

"Yes. It's her pet name for me. Or it was."

"I see. And what did you say?"

"I said, 'oh'. I was too shocked to say anything else."

"And what did she say?"

Albert now looked gloomier than ever. "She asked if I would like to join them."

Clive raised an eyebrow. "Well … she's more broadminded than I expected!" He paused. "So, what are you going to do about it? How are you going to get her back?"

"I'm not. I can't compete with someone who works in a sewage works. I have reconciled myself. It is my destiny to live a life of loneliness and misery."

"But you have me," said Clive, consolingly.

"As I said, my destiny is loneliness and misery. I just have to accept that nothing will change until I end up at the Great Recycle Centre in the sky. I thought Victoria and I had something going together but I don't know what it's all about anymore."

At that moment he noted a fleeting twinkle in Clive's eye. "No. Just don't. I'm not in the mood."

But it was too late. Clive had decided on a song and was not going to be stopped.

Albie

What's it all about, Albie?
Is it just for the garbage they bring?
What's it all about - when they chuck it out, Albie?
Are we meant to take all that they give?

Or are we meant to say no?
They say that love is blind, Albie
But you'll end up in some sort of hell
If love also has no sense of smell, Albie

When she chucks you out, Albie
Will it help if you scream and you shout?
Or if you believe - there's a heaven above, Albie
It may help you to recycle love
Then maybe you'll find love again, Albie
Albie

"Er, thank you," said Albert insincerely, when the embarrassment of it was over.

Clive stared at him again. "I have one more question."

"What?"

"Have you had the call?"

"The call?"

"Yes. The call. The call. The one where she phones to officially dump you."

"No. She wouldn't do that. She would tell me face to face. I'm sure of it."

Albert was trying to sound confident but failing. Then his mobile phone rang. He identified the caller and mouthed to Clive that it was Victoria, while it kept ringing.

Clive gave another hard stare. "Well? Are you going to answer it?"

Albert reluctantly did so and listened intently.

Clive only heard one side of the conversation but Albert seemed to keep repeating what Victoria was telling him as if he were some kind of a Zombie.

"You want to bring Frank round to my place later? O...kay."

"You think the three of us could come up with some interesting ideas?"

"You think I should get to know Frank more intimately? But I don't know him at all!"

"Oh."

"Oh."

"I see."

"I understand. Yes. I'll see you both later."

By the time the call ended, Albert was smiling again. Clive waited for an explanation.

"Frank is Victoria's brother-in-law. She thought I knew about him. She wants the three of us to discuss arranging a surprise party for her sister's birthday."

Clive shook his head. "You idiot."

"Yes, I suppose I am."

"You really should be more thankful for what you've got, Albert. Your love life is fine. You have nothing to worry about. You found somebody. Victoria. Spare a thought for poor Ted. He was telling me that being overweight means he's never had a girlfriend. He said he tried the regular dating sites but never had any luck. He eventually found hope when he joined a dating site that specialised in finding a match for the larger person. The site was called XXXLove.com. He was encouraged by the blurb from the site creator whose site slogan was '*Big man, big woman, big love.*'

The lady who created the site was large herself and started it due to her own similar experiences. In her intro she said, 'The women on this site are not looking for men to sweep us off our feet. That might cause them a serious injury, but we are looking for romance and restaurants … Come to XXXLove and find your chubby bunny.'

"Did he find his chubby bunny in the end?" asked Albert.

"No. They told him he wasn't fat enough for the XXXL crowd and suggested he found an XXL site."

"So what did he do?"

"He began eating more cakes."

"I see what you're doing," said Albert.

"What?"

"You're trying to cheer me up by talking about somebody whose love-life is more messed up than mine."

"Is it working?"

"It shouldn't be, but yes. You know," said Albert, now in a much better mood, "I've been thinking about those Swedish talking recycle bins and I think we should have the same here. If we had one, I have some ideas what they might say."

Clive was pleased. The old Albert was returning.

"Go on then," he encouraged.

"How about…

You're trying to put that item in the wrong opening.

Or … I love your junk.

Or … more please, don't stop."

Clive interrupted. "How about, next time bring a friend? Or, that item is much too long to fit inside."

They were both laughing. Clive was happy. Albert now seemed like a new man … just like his old self.

Sgt. Pill Popper's Lonely Hearts

Fun fact: Around 22 million items of fixable furniture, 11,000 busted bikes and 28 million trashed toys are thrown away in the UK each year.

Every day, when Clive Dumper and Albert Riddle headed toward their favourite bench across the road from the recycle centre to take their lunch break, they walked past a large shipping container. The container housed a variety of items left by the public which were considered to be reusable. The facility was frequented by many and customers would often take home such items and give them another life.

The container stood close to the entrance gates for the public's convenience. It was generally a place of quiet browsing. Today however, as Albert and Clive walked by, there were sounds of some kind of kerfuffle coming from inside.

Jabby came running out of it, arms waving frantically to get their attention.

"Help!" He shouted. "There are two wild, out of control grannies in here fighting for a child's bike." He looked visibly shaken.

Clive observed there were two electric disability scooters parked outside of the container.

He laughed. "Grannies?! What are they fighting with? Their handbags?"

"No. They are waving their crutches around. They're dangerous. I tried to break them up and they both whacked me." He rubbed his shin then his shoulder and grimaced.

Clive looked to Albert, the senior man, to see if he would get involved.

"I'm not well," said Albert. "I have every confidence that you can deal with a couple of grannies. Tell them fighting is not allowed on the premises and if they don't stop, you'll call the police."

They walked on, leaving Jabby to limp back inside still rubbing his shoulder.

* * *

The two men, like homing pigeons, found their way to their bench and began to eat their sandwiches. Clive was first to speak.

"What's wrong with you?"

"What do you mean?"

"You just said you weren't well. And you clearly did not want to get involved in the granny dispute. That's not like you. Normally you can't wait to give a granny a helping hand. You get on so well with the female over seventies demographic."

Clive was grinning, hoping for a reaction but Albert ignored the comment.

"I twinged my back at the weekend and had to take some Ibuprofen."

Clive was puzzled. "You didn't seem to have any difficulty shifting the trash this morning."

"No. The tablets worked. The trouble with Ibuprofen is that it gives you … other problems."

"Ah," Clive nodded knowingly. But before he could come up with some smart comment, Jabby's two grannies rode out of the recycle centre on their scooters, side by side and easily identifiable by their crutches. One granny had painted her crutches bright pink while the other had traditional silver ones. Both had their crutches clipped to the backs of their scooters.

Albert looked pleased. "Well done Jabby," he said. "The old dears have resolved their differences."

Clive shook his head. "I don't think so. Look at their expressions. I doubt they've lined up their scooters for a 'Gran' Prix!"

It was true. Their expressions looked a tad confrontational. Granny Pink was clearly mouthing something at granny Silver, but an impression can easily be misinterpreted. Especially bearing in mind they could barely hear them from their bench. However, when read in conjunction with their body language, well … It is difficult to read the body language of fist shaking as anything other than there may be a soupcon of animosity at play.

Albert did not wish to admit it. "We're looking at two lovely grannies. I don't accept that grannies can be truly aggressive."

Clive shook his head.

"You couldn't be more wrong. As a child, I mostly only ever saw my own grandmothers separately, but there was this one time, when my parents had both of them around together for afternoon tea. You wouldn't believe the carnage left after they both pounced on the last Hobnob. The biscuit tin was left broken and dented and the only indication that there had ever been a full biscuit in there was a thin layer of crushed crumbs. And that wasn't the worst of it. Both grandmothers left the house with bandages on their hands. It was brutal." He shuddered in remembrance of the incident.

"Well, you're wrong about these grannies," said Albert. "Look, they are moving apart."

Granny Silver stayed put by the gate while Granny Pink scooted off down the pavement. The tension having subsided, Albert took a pack of pills from his pocket and swallowed a couple with the remains of his tea.

"Not more pills," said Clive. "How many have you had?"

Albert held his stomach and looked a bit desperate. "Probably not enough. I don't want to talk about it."

They resumed their lunch in silence, while keeping half an eye on the granny situation. Granny Pink had scooted away some distance but stopped and turned around when granny Silver shouted something. Clive could not hear what was said because the silence on the bench was broken by a disturbing noise emanating from somewhere about Albert's person. Clive said nothing but shuffled to the end of the bench. Albert was acutely aware of the problem and shuffled to the opposite end, wishing not so much to avoid overwhelming Clive's sensibilities, as to avoid overwhelming his own.

They now looked decidedly like bench bookends. There were no books, but Clive had brought with him the latest copy of Recycling Monthly from the office. He flicked through the pages finding nothing noteworthy with which to begin a new conversation until, near the end of the magazine, his interest was piqued by something and he laughed out loud.

"This is new," he said, "they have a new section here with lonely-hearts ads."

"What's funny about that?"

"These are lonely-hearts ads for 'green' people."

"Green people? You mean like aliens, Little Green Men?" Joked Albert.

"No, I mean green like in people who do recycling and want to save the planet."

"Makes sense," said Albert, thoughtfully. "You don't want to meet your true love, only to find that they never separate their Styrofoam from their recyclable plastic. Styrofoam takes 500 years to break down in a landfill you know."

"Of course, I know. I do work here."

"Oh, yeah. Why don't you read one out?"

At this point their conversation was interrupted by the volume of vindictive verbiage coming from the duelling grannies.

Clive decided to ignore them and scanned a few of the ads to pick out an example. He raised his voice to be heard above the latest kerfuffle.

"Here's one.

Green-fingered Male, 45, has own greenhouse, seeks Female for sowing wild oats and practice pricking-out together. Proficient at bedding, in the borders, on the allotment. Anywhere really."

They both giggled.

"Surely that's a joke," said Albert.

"I don't think so. How about this one from a woman?

Attractive female, some say woman … some say green goddess. Would like to meet male eco warrior. Must be organic, sustainable and ultimately … compostable. To share days out at recycling centres, beach clean-ups and the occasional environmental marches. Anyone ignorant of the seven types of recyclable plastics need not apply."

"That's crazy," said Albert, "who would want to go out with someone like that?"

"Says someone who spends most of his days at a recycle centre! Maybe that green-fingered male I just mentioned? Anyway, have you ever thought of using the Lonely-Hearts column yourself?"

Albert scratched the stubble on his chin.

"There was this one time when I was in my early twenties. I was working at B&Q back then but still living at home. I was trying to prove to my parents that I was a fully functioning adult and could maintain a relationship."

Clive laughed. "Fully functioning adult? You're barely one of those even now! Anyway, what happened? How many responses did you get?"

"If you're going to mock me, I'm not going to tell you."

Clive looked suitably contrite, just enough to encourage Albert to spill the beans.

"Well alright. As long as you promise not to laugh."

"I promise, I promise," said Clive gleefully.

"Well, I didn't have a girlfriend back then so I thought I would try the Lonely-Hearts column in the local newspaper."

"Do you remember what you wrote?"

"No."

"Did you get any replies?"

"No."

"So, what did you do?"

"I put the ad in again."

"And?"

"Same result."

Clive looked miffed. "Well, that was a boring story."

"I did get a reply eventually." Albert paused. "After 19 ads."

Clive looked interested again and tried not to laugh. "Tell me. Who was the vision of loveliness who agreed to go out with you?"

"It wasn't a girl."

Clive's eyes opened wide. "You got a reply from a guy!?"

"No. It was from my mother."

Clive's eyes opened wider. "Your mother was looking for a date!?"

"No. She knew it was me. She just wanted to remind me to get some bread on my way home from B&Q."

Throughout all of this the grannies had scooted to meet each other again face to face. After some kind of heated conversation and more fist waving, they moved back to their previous positions to face each other at a distance. Each granny held a single crutch in their right hands, their left hands on the scooter controls. Suddenly they stuffed their crutches under their arms holding them horizontally, rubber ends pointing at each other.

Clive pulled out his mobile. "This looks like it is going to get out of hand."

"Are you phoning the police?"

"No."

"Are you going over there to break them up?"

"No chance. I'm calling Jabby."

Albert watched in horror as Granny Pink and Granny Silver set off toward each other at full speed looking for all the world like jousting medieval knights. If this was a game of chicken it only half worked. Fortunately, the effort of holding out their "lances" became too much for them and they both dropped their crutches before they could cause any personal injury. Sadly, they could not control their "horses" either. At least not sufficiently to stop them barrelling into each other. There was a clatter as both scooters met then overturned leaving a pile of twisted metal, plastic and grannies in the middle of the pavement.

Luckily Jabby, Bogsy, and Ms Hunter came running out to sort out the mess.

Albert clutched his stomach again and looked most uncomfortable. He turned to Clive.

"I need a distraction. Do you have some silly song of yours about fighting grannies?"

"I probably should, but no. However, I was thinking about those pills of yours. And pills in general. There seems to be a pill for everything these days. We probably all take too many. But we love them. Want to hear it?"

"I know I'll regret it, but go on then."

My Favourite Pills

Steroids and statins and other life savers
Could be the cause of my strangest behaviours
Bright coloured tablets to cure all my ills
These are a few of my favourite pills

When the blues strike
When the bills land
When I start to drown
I grab my prescription for favourite pills
Then I don't feel so down

Ketamine, codeine and cocaine and caffeine
Slipped in champagne with a measure of morphine
Then I forget all my fevers and chills
With just a few of these favourite pills

When the blues strike
When the bills land
When I've got no dough
I grab my prescription for favourite pills
Then I don't feel so low

They say Ibuprofen is good medication
Though sometimes a side-effect's bad constipation
But getting things moving is one of my skills
That's when I reach for my favourite pills

When the runs start
When I feel loose
Feel a movement grow
No time to pop any favourite pills
Not when I need to go

Albert clutched his stomach again. He got up with a quick "Sorry but have to dash", running across the road toward the toilet at remarkable speed, narrowly missing an oncoming ambulance.

Identity Crisis

A shaft of spring sunshine slipped through the office window, bounced off the bright dungarees of Ms Hunter and cast an orange glow upon the faces of the assembled recycle centre workers. Eschewing her usual meditative manoeuvres, she simply stood in front of her desk holding a large brown envelope.

"Thank you all for coming to this special staff meeting. I have been requested by head office to make a special announcement as contained in this envelope."

The muffled groan from her audience was not encouraging. She wafted the envelope in the air in a vague effort to emphasize its importance. Her audience seemed unmoved. She opened the envelope and pulled out some papers. Glancing at the title of the memo caused her to sigh inwardly. A very important message to all staff? In her experience, there was an inverse correlation between the stated importance of any head office memo and its actual importance. Nevertheless, she read it out in as neutral a voice as she could manage.

"Message to all workers. It has come to our attention that the council policy relating to personal identity is inadequate. In fact, there has been no policy on this matter at all.

The Council recognises that staff who are able to be themselves in work are more likely to enjoy going to work, feel included, and can achieve their full potential. As an inclusive organisation, the Council is committed to the health, well-being and dignity of all our staff, regardless of their gender identity and expression. The Council strives, through this policy and guidance and other relevant workplace policies (including our Equality Opportunity Policy and our Grievance and Disciplinary Procedures) to create an environment where all our employees are engaged, happy and productive. We will not tolerate discrimination, victimisation or harassment on the basis of any grounds, including a person's transgender status, gender identity or gender expression.

Pronouns are words we use to refer to people's gender in conversation. Examples of pronouns include I, me, mine, he/she, his/her, herself, they/them, we, us, ours and ourselves. Some people use gender-neutral language like they/their. Asking someone which pronouns they use can help to avoid making assumptions and potentially getting it wrong.

Anyway, the gist of all this is that we must respect how people wish to self-identify. If anybody here wishes to state for the record how they would like to be addressed then I need to make a note of it."

She looked around the room and saw Bogsy put up his be-puppeted hand. Squeaking in his high voice he said, "Would it be ok with everybody if they referred to me as 'The Hand'?"

"Of course, Bogsy. Erm, I mean of course Hand."

"The Hand thanks you."

She thought about this for a moment then said, "Does 'The Hand' have a gender preference?"

"Of course not," said The Hand. "That would be crazy." Bogsy's mouth suddenly stretched into a wide grin. This was so unusual that Ms Hunter remarked on how pleased she was to see it.

"It's just that I'm happy I'm being taken seriously for a change. Nobody ever takes me seriously."

Ms Hunter looked around the room. "Any other questions?"

"This is ridiculous. What about someone who self identifies as serial killer? Do we have to respect that too?" said Clive.

Ms Hunter shook her head, looked upwards as if seeking guidance from the serene Buddha, but not receiving any, turned her gaze on Clive and fixed him with her zen-most look of disapproval.

"Look Clive, I'm as doubtful about all of this as you are but we don't run this organisation, so if we want to keep collecting our wages, we have to go along with it."

"I'm not entirely sure that that is true," said Clive. "You are the only person here who expressed their identity preference from day one."

"What do you mean?"

"I mean it's not Miss Hunter or Mrs Hunter. You prefer to be called Ms Hunter."

"Well yes, but that's different."

"Is it though? Is it really? The only difference is that where some people now want to express some information about themselves, your choice of honorific is designed to hide some information about yourself."

"Be that as it may, I will need you all to let me know how you wish to be addressed so I can report back to head office."

Clive frowned. "I think we all need to think carefully about this. How long have we got?"

Ms Hunter sighed. "I suppose if you get back to me by lunchtime it will be alright. Oh, and one more thing everybody. Apparently, we need a volunteer for the position of 'Inclusivity Representative' in case any of our customers have issues. First person to volunteer gets the job."

She sensed from the silence, a possible lack of enthusiasm for the position so added, "And a cream bun."

* * *

"Well," mumbled Clive after he bit into his cheese sandwich. "Have you decided how you want to self-identify yet? What pronouns etc?"

Albert was looking blankly into space.

"Well?"

"Well, what?"

"Well, what are you thinking?"

Albert's intent gaze never wavered from the view of the recycle centre from the bench where they both sat.

"I was thinking - what should I have for tea tonight …"

Clive, eager for Albert to engage, persisted.

"I am asking you what you think about the world of 'woke' we seem to be living in these days? Surely you must have an opinion."

Albert shrugged. "I try not to have opinions. They can get you into trouble. I suppose I could never be like those woke people though. I'm tired all the time."

If Clive's head was a cartoon, there would have been steam coming out of his ears.

Albert decided to put Clive out of his misery.

"Even though I try not to have opinions I know what you mean. My aunt Lucy's granddaughter is only 8 years old and quite short. She recently told Lucy that she decided to self-identify as a tall 18-year-old. So that, quote, they will have to let me drink alcohol in the pub and go on the big rides at the fair."

"That's what I'm talking about!" exclaimed Clive, nodding his head vigorously and gearing up for a rant. "The point is, if you are a fat slob of a man and decide to self-identify as slim and fit, you're still never going to be a babe magnet. And you'll still get stuck in revolving doors. It's like me saying my TV self-identifies as a microwave to avoid paying the licence fee.

Look, only the other day I was reading that university students these days refuse to allow controversial external speakers if they think they are likely to hear something they disagree with. I think they call it no-platforming. I mean, whatever happened to free speech? And I'm a great believer in free speech because, well, without free speech, how would we know who the stupid people are?"

Albert interrupted his flow. "So, what should the students do when they hear someone making objectionable comments?"

"They should do what students used to do in the last century. The students would listen very politely but at the end they would express their disapproval by hurling rotten fruit and veg at the speakers as they took their bows. A much more positive approach than no-platforming them. But the whole identity thing now permeates the whole of society. You must have come across it yourself."

Albert scratched his chin stubble, thinking. "Oh, do you mean like that new café they opened on the High Street? The owners were too scared to put the usual images of a man and a woman on the toilet doors so instead they have a Sausage and an Egg. Is that the sort of thing you mean?"

"Erm … yes … possibly … well … maybe. I was thinking more along the lines of …" Clive's eyes darted about, searching for another example. "For example, did you hear that in the next Star Wars movie, one of the robots is going to be called R2-Me2? That's the sort of thing I'm talking about. Anyway, the main thing is, have you decided on how you would like to be addressed?"

Albert nodded.

"In that case let's go find Ms Hunter so she can finalise her report."

* * *

As Albert and Clive were entering the office, Bogsy was leaving and looking rather pleased with himself. Ms Hunter was sat at her desk filling in a form but looked up as they entered.

"Good," she said. "You are the last two. But before you say anything I should mention that Bogsy just volunteered to be our 'Inclusivity Representative', so that option is off the table. Now, before you start, I am warning you both, I am at my wit's end with all this. I already have Bogsy referring to himself as The Hand, Ted wants to be identified as The Cream Bun and Jabby would like to be referred to as The Stud. Now tell me, have you decided how you would like to be addressed?"

Albert stepped forward. "I would like to be addressed as Lord of the Dump."

Ms Hunter stared at him. "And what about you Clive? I suppose you want to be addressed as Prime Minister?"

"Not at all. You may simply refer to me as 'Your Majesty'."

Ms Hunter looked to the heavens. "Oh, my lord," she muttered.

"Yes?" said Albert. "How can I help you?"

She lowered her head to her desk and banged her forehead softly against the wood. When she eventually raised it, she took the form and papers from head office, ripped them up and tossed the remains into the bin. She then focussed on Albert and Clive.

"If anyone asks. We never received this. Never even heard of it. And even if we did, it must have been accidentally recycled. None of this happened and you are not lords or majesties. Got it?"

They both nodded affirmatively.

As they were leaving, an irate customer barged through the door. If Albert and Clive were to comment upon the customer's gender they would have had to say, 'undecided'. Undecided marched up to Ms Hunter and demanded to see the centre's 'Inclusivity Representative'.

Ms Hunter rose, smiled sweetly and said, "Follow me, allow me introduce you to one of our hands."

Albert and Clive, eager to tag along and see the outcome of this proposed introduction, bumped shoulders together as they both tried to get through the office door at the same time. They both took a step backward.

Clive laughed and making an exaggerated, low bow to Albert, gesticulated at the door and said, "After you, My Lord."

Albert also laughed. He reciprocated with an even lower bow. "No, no. After you, Your Majesty."

Purple Urkle

The weekly Monday staff meeting at the Dedbury Recycling Centre was about to start. Everybody sat waiting for the meeting to begin. Everybody except for Bogsy. Bogsy was late. He was often late since being transferred to Dedbury on a permanent basis. It was understandable. He lived in the next town.

In the meantime, Ms Hunter, as was her habit, practised some of her yoga exercises while waiting for all the staff to arrive. The gathered congregation watched in rapt fascination, studying her improbable contortions. She began by lying flat on her back on the desktop in her bright orange dungarees. Then, bringing her legs up by her head, she snaked her arms around them, just above her now prominent rear. Finally, she lodged her ankles under her shoulders and her crossed feet became a pillow for her head.

Her rear end, over which the dungarees now stretched tightly, now hovered slightly above the desktop, creating an image of a floating orb of orange.

The onlookers stared at that magnificent moon, admiring her derriere in reverential silence. Albert however, after a meditative moment, believed the onlookers admiration might be too reverential. He became a little uncomfortable and felt the need to break the silence with an observation.

"That is a very …er, interesting position."

"Yes Albert. Well observed. The position is an aid to meditation. It is supposed to help with one's concentration. Do you think it helps with concentration?"

Albert studied her area of orangey rotundity. "Yes," he said, "I think my concentration is definitely improved."

The all-male onlookers nodded in enthusiastic agreement.

"That's good," she said. "Here's my thought for the day ... All that we are, is the result of what we have thought. The mind is everything. What we think, we become."

"What we think, we become," Albert repeated. He stared at her contorted position again. "I can't imagine what you must be thinking. Does the position have a name?"

Unseen behind her behind, Ms Hunter smiled, pleased at the interest. "Yes. The position is called 'Dwi Pada Sirsasana'. It means 'both legs behind the head' in Hindi. It is a new move I have been practising. It is also supposed to help increase blood flow. What do you think?"

Albert searched the faces of the onlookers. "I think ... blood flow ... is definitely increasing," he said, supportively.

The onlookers, to a man, nodded in agreement, this time even more enthusiastically.

"You should try it, Albert."

Before he could respond, the moment was broken by the entrance of an agitated Bogsy. His stocky, six-foot three body barged into the room like a man desperate to impart important news. But try as he might, he could not speak. He thrust his hand onto a bulge in his trouser pocket and pulled out his hand puppet. The puppet still matched Bogsy's facial features even down to the stubble on his chin and the scar on his left cheek. As soon as he placed it over his right hand, he tried to speak again but still could not.

Clive pointed to the woolly hat Bogsy was wearing and his scarred face relaxed with a broad grin of understanding. He reached into his pocket again, this time pulling out a tiny replica of the hat he was wearing. The second he placed this on the head of his hand puppet he was able to speak, albeit in his usual high-pitched squeak.

"There's going to be a strike! Refuse workers!"

A loud groan echoed around the room.

Ms Hunter untangled her arms and legs as he was making his announcement. She looked puzzled.

"Is that a problem?"

"Big problem," said Clive. He turned to Bogsy. "When does it start?"

"Tomorrow," squeaked Bogsy."

The room groaned again.

"I don't understand," she said.

Clive explained. "The last time they announced a bin strike in advance, the entire town decided to bring in their rubbish the day before. We should prepare for a tsunami of trash."

"Too late," squeaked Bogsy. "The tidal wave has reached the gate. The queue is already half a mile long."

"What can we do?" asked Ms Hunter.

Clive thought about it. "The public will mainly be bringing in their black binbags. We need to allocate all available skip capacity to them. But it won't be enough. This is going to be terrible. Last time this happened, the black bins contained more than their fair share of dirty nappies. Anyone who emerged from the experience unscathed earned themselves the nickname 'Poodini'."

Ms Hunter frowned at him. "I don't want to hear any more of your usual negativity and pessimism Clive."

"Well, we're not going to solve our problems by wishful thinking."

"No, of course not. What I say is this. The pessimist complains about the wind; the optimist expects it to change; the realist adjusts the sails. We are not going to give up without a fight. We are going to adjust our sails. This is what we do. All staff concentrate only on general waste. Set up an extra skip for black bags. Compress what we can as it comes in and if it can't be compressed then we pile it high."

"And how are we going to pile it high?" asked Clive.

"When it gets too high to throw them in then you and Albert climb onto the skip and make sure the bags are placed on the pile carefully. If necessary, you climb the pile as it rises. Now, that's the plan."

Clive shook his head, about to say something negative. "But ..."

Ms Hunter interrupted, shaking a Zen-infused finger at him. "I don't want to hear it Clive. Now, we have 20 minutes before we open, have you anything positive to say? A few words of encouragement before we start."

Clive thought about it. "Maybe a rousing song?"

"Uh oh," said Albert.

Ms Hunter frowned but nodded agreement, giving him a final warning. "Remember Clive, positivity."

There are Bins Comin' in

There are bins comin' in
We love it when we're near 'em
They come from all over the town
They rustle when you hear 'em
And it's our job to clear 'em
Take 'em in, stack 'em up, squash 'em down
There are bins comin' in
There are bins comin' in right now

They deliver us garbage of beauty
In cars that could burst at the seems
To shift it is our bounden duty
Recycling! The job of our dreams

"A little less sarcasm please," interjected Ms Hunter.

There are bins comin' in
And each bag someone throws
Can be fragile and easily rip
It may seem to your nose
Someone dirtied their clothes
But we smile, chuck the pile, in a skip
There are bins comin' in
There are bins comin' in right now

They're bringing their bottles and cardboard
Their plastic, their metal, their wood
There's nothing they wouldn't recycle
Their old underwear if they could

There are bins comin' in
The flow never ending
Like a river overflowing its banks
And the crap they are sending
We shall soon be befriending
And for this we must all give our thanks
There are bins comin' in
There are bins comin' in right now

They bring us disposable nappies
Some filled with brown coloured goo
But still, we are all happy chappies
Though sometimes it leaks onto you

"Positive Clive, positive."

So much love comin' in
We should bottle it or can it
From people all over the land
They want to save the planet

But they know that they cannot
So we're here ... to give them ... all a hand
There are bins comin' in
There are bins comin' in right now

They're bringing us every sad item
Gathering dust in their homes
They bring them in ad infinitum
Every thing every one of them owns

There are bins comin' in
There are bins comin' in right now

"Very good Clive. Now let's get to it. And everybody, remember what I said. The mind is everything. What we think, we become."

"I hope not. Not based on what I'm thinking," said Clive.

* * *

The staff dispersed, two skips were prepared, the gates were opened and the cars came flooding in. Not only were there cars, but a fair number of people (presumably folk who lived close by) had come on foot. Some were pushing their wheelie bins and a few were carrying their bin bags, a couple in each hand.

Albert and Clive stood by general waste and prepared to accept incoming.

"What were you thinking?" asked Albert. "Because I was thinking of something too."

"Eh?"

"Back there. In the office."

"Oh, I was thinking of a giant orange moon."

Albert nodded. "Me too. Was yours a male moon or a female moon?"

"A female moon."

"Mine too."

The two men spent a moment with their own private thoughts before readying themselves for the first wave of binbags.

* * *

Albert and Clive each took a small step ladder with them to the skip they would use for the first load of binbags. They would need to climb up later and get on top of them. The plan seemed clear but events took an odd turn, right from the start. Amongst the first dozen cars to unload, was a man in his thirties and wearing a grey jumper who tipped his black bags in then took a homemade flag on a stick from his car, climbed Clive's stepladders and started waving it about.

"What's that on his flag?" asked Albert.

"I don't believe I'm saying this, but it looks like an image of a dustbin," said Clive.

The dustbin was also grey, matching the colour of his jumper. The man soon gathered the attention of other drivers and proceedings ground to an immediate halt.

"What do we do?" asked Albert.

"Nothing," said Clive. "I'm interested to see where this is going."

Once he had people's attention, flag man began speaking with passion, from the top of the ladders.

"*Fellow citizens!*
We fight for our right to live
To exist without trash blocking our doorways
Without the stench of rotting food
Without potential diseases at our gates

*Without the likelihood of rats attacking our children
We will not be stopped
We will not stay quietly at home
We will survive this strike
We will get in our cars
We will load them with binbags
We will bring them to the recycling centre ourselves
Today, we celebrate our Bin-dependence Day!"*

There was a huge round of applause then he got back in his car and drove away.

"At least he didn't say he would fight on the beaches," said Clive. "Let's get to work."

Throughout the day, the bags just kept coming.

* * *

When the bags reached the rim of the skip, Albert and Clive climbed in at opposite ends. But when Albert jumped in, he thought he heard a rustling noise emanating from a few binbags below him. He became agitated.

"Clive. Did you hear that? The binbags moved. I think there's a rat down there. I hate rats."

"I heard nothing. Calm down. You're imagining it. And how do you even know it's a rat? It could be anything."

"It's a rat. I can smell it."

"You can smell a rat? You're crazy. That's what years of working in a toxic environment does to you."

"No. I can smell it. It's my superpower."

"You have a superpower that lets you aromatically detect a rat?" Clive laughed.

"I don't care what you think. There's a rat in here." Albert stamped his foot around hoping to force the rat out of hiding.

Nothing moved. But he was convinced there was one. He decided to put the rat on notice.

"Message to any rats down there, go away. I'm warning you. Don't come anywhere near me. I'm a trained ninja you know. What do you say to that? If you're down there, then come on. Fight me if you dare."

Clive gave Albert a hard stare. "You do realise you're talking to a non-existent rat? More than that, you are talking crazy to a non-existent rat. And why do you hate rats anyway?"

"I sat on one as a child and it bit me."

"Oh? Where?"

"In the kitchen. So I want to get as far away from the rat as possible. That means moving upwards."

Albert turned to his fellow workmates. "Everybody, throw up binbags. As fast as you can. I need to climb higher."

* * *

The main skip filled up early on, but Albert and Clive managed to compress them then pile them, pyramid fashion, by climbing up the bags as the pile rose, as planned. By lunchtime they could not get the pile any higher and a fresh skip was started. They took the opportunity to take a break and wandered off to sit on their usual bench outside the centre to eat their sandwiches.

Albert stared morosely at the endless queue of cars, all bursting with binbags, waiting to get in. He studied the faces of the drivers as they inched by. Expressions baked with irritation at having to be there, but dusted with sprinkles of smugness for having beaten the strike.

"Don't you think people do crazy things sometimes? Haven't they got anything better to do? Look at all these cars."

"It is only in times of crisis that you discover what is truly important to people," said Clive. "What about that guy who was inspired to make a speech about it? But you never know what's important to people."

"What do you mean?" mumbled a distracted Albert, through his mouthful of cheese and bread.

"For example, during the pandemic, we learned that the overwhelmingly most important thing to people wasn't say ... getting bread or milk, it was getting toilet rolls. And now we hear there is the possibility of a bin collection strike, getting rid of their trash is top priority. I suspect that any politician running on guaranteed bin collections and toilet rolls would win by a landslide."

Albert did not respond. First, he was thinking about a landslide of binbags and toilet rolls, but then he was thinking of something else. He kept staring ahead, but not at the cars anymore. He seemed lost in his thoughts. And not happy thoughts by the look of him.

"Come on," said Clive. "You look worried. Tell me. What's bothering you?"

"I'm worried that I might be a bad person."

Clive gave him a hard stare. "That sounds like something one of your priests might better advise you on rather than me."

"I might well do that at my next confession, but if I tell you what happened, maybe you could let me know what you think."

"Go on then." Clive was intrigued.

"Well, I was reading this news story about some American guy who has been accused of murdering his wife."

"Tragic."

"Yes, a real tragedy, but when I read the story, I couldn't stop laughing. That's why I think I must be a bad person."

"Tell me about it and I'll give you my opinion."

"Okay, thanks. Anyway, this guy is called Brian Walshe and as I said, he has been arrested for murdering his wife."

"Doesn't sound very funny so far," said Clive.

"The police think the wife may have been killed, dismembered, bagged and thrown into a skip."

Clive grimaced. "Sounds even less funny now. Where is this going?"

"Well, there was a pre court hearing where some of the evidence against him was revealed. The prosecution was able to get hold of the records of some of his recent Google searches."

Albert pulled out his phone and scrolled through to a news article listing some of the searches.

"Listen to some of these."

"How to stop a body from decomposing?"

"10 ways to dispose of a dead body if you really need to"

"How long for someone to be missing before you can inherit?"

Clive laughed out loud.

"Wait. There's more," said Albert.

"How to clean blood from a wooden floor?"

"What is the rate of decomposition of a body found in a plastic bag compared to on a surface in the woods?"

Albert looked up to see Clive's reaction. "Shall I go on?"

Clive's face had turned an unusual shade of green. He had stopped laughing and had stopped eating his sandwich.

"You could have waited for me to finish my lunch."

"Sorry," said Albert. "Apparently the husband was also seen on surveillance video buying $450 worth of cleaning supplies, including mops, buckets, tarpaulins, tape and other items, at a home improvement store on the day after his wife was last seen."

Clive shook his head. "You are not a bad person, my friend. If you were a bad person, I would be too ... because I also laughed. I suppose the moral of your story is be careful what you google." He had recovered enough to take another bite of his sandwich. "Maybe we should all worry about that. Sometimes you could google something innocently but it could be misinterpreted. I mean, for example, what was the last thing you googled?"

He took another bite of his sandwich while Albert thought about it.

Albert mulled it over. I can't remember. "Let me see." He flicked around on his phone till he got to the search history. Hmm, yes, I remember now. It was ... 'Why do I have green poo?'

Clive choked on his sandwich and a big chunk of cheese fell out of his mouth and rolled under the bench.

Albert looked from the cheese to Clive in an accusatory manner.

"If you think I am picking that up you are mistaken. It will be filthy now. What you should be doing, is explaining why you have green poo."

"Oh, it's not my poo. It belongs to Victoria's sister's toddler, Noah."

"So why did you google as if it was yours?"

"I thought if I googled 'Why does Noah have green poo?' it might sound a bit weird."

Clive gave Albert another hard stare.

"You know ... I really worry about you sometimes. So why does Noah have green poo?"

"The doctors didn't know. But they later discovered he'd drunk three large, green Slush Puppies while he was out with his granddad."

Clive nodded. "Okay. But that was a weird one-off. What else did you google recently?"

Albert scratched the stubble on his chin and checked the next item in his search history. "I guess that would be 'Why don't dogs have belly buttons?'"

Clive stared at him again.

"Before you ask, I was googling it on behalf of my aunt Lucy."

"Dogs are mammals, aren't they? Surely, they do have belly buttons."

"No, they don't. But I'd better not tell you why yet because the reason is disgusting and you still haven't finished your sandwich."

"Okay then. But those two searches were on behalf of other people. I want to know something you actually searched for yourself."

Albert thumbed the screen of his phone again and read the next item in his search history.

"Why isn't eleven pronounced onety-one?"

Clive stared again and shook his head. "Well, you're not going to be arrested for googling that. But perhaps you should be."

* * *

By the time they got back to work, the second skip was almost filled to the rim. Albert and Clive jumped inside and by catching and positioning the bags as they were thrown up from below, gradually rose higher on a rising tide of trash. The only lull came late afternoon when the cars eased off. By this time, they were both at the top of a black plastic pyramid. They took a break, sitting next to each other on the top few bags. Albert took out his vape and began blowing smoke everywhere. Clive immediately began coughing.

"What on earth are you smoking?"

"One of the new 'special' flavours. It's called Purple Urkle. They say, 'puff the Purple Urkle and forget all your troubles'.

Clive looked it up on his phone and was shocked. "I hope you didn't buy this online. It says here it's illegal in this country. Where did you get it?"

"Some guy in the pub. He said it had medicinal properties." He puffed the Purple Urkle again, inhaling deeply.

"Medicinal properties?!" Exclaimed Clive. "This stuff could kill you! And not only that, you made me google it, so now I'm probably on some police watch list!" He reached across and swiped at the vape. It fell from Albert's hand and tumbled down the black mountain, completely lost from sight.

"Hey! I paid good money for that."

"You should be thanking me for saving your life."

"Well, I should be really annoyed with you, but for some reason I'm feeling quite good right now so I'll get my own back by telling you why dogs don't have belly buttons.

So, it's like this. When puppies are born, each one is still inside their own fluid-filled sac. The mother dog needs to tear open the sac and lick the puppy clean. She also needs to chew off the umbilical cord, leaving behind a tiny remnant that will dry up and fall away a few days later. Over the next few days, the stump dries up and falls off. The only remaining evidence is a small flat scar, the belly button. So, technically they do have belly buttons, but a lot of people think they don't because they are barely visible."

"Then I was right all along when I said dogs must have belly buttons."

"Er, yes," agreed Albert reluctantly. "But it annoys me when you are right all the time, so that's why I disagreed with you … temporarily."

Clive sighed.

By the end of the afternoon the river of cars reduced to a trickle then dried up altogether as the light began to fade. The recycle centre workers had been commended by Ms Hunter for a job well done and now only Albert and Clive remained to lock up and leave.

If they were still annoyed with each other, it did not show and all was well with the world.

"Fancy going to the pub later?" Asked Clive.

"I would, but it's vaccine night at the clinic. I have to go get my Covid booster jab. Maybe tomorrow."

As he was locking the gate, the security lights came on by timer. The twin peaks of the binbag mountains glistened with golden reflections. Albert paused a moment to take in the wonder of it.

"It's kind of glorious," he said.

"Ha!" laughed Clive. "That doesn't sound like the Albert I know. That's the Purple Urkle talking."

Albert turned around to lock the gate and saw, in his peripheral vision, something small and furry run past him heading for the skips.

"Did you see that?"

"See what?"

"I definitely saw a couple of rats this time."

"Definitely the Purple Urkle," said Clive.

* * *

Later that evening, on top of Binbag Mountain sat two rats in silhouette, courtesy of one of the security lights. In silhouette, they both looked black. One of them held a chunk of cheese. The other one held a small device. Each rat seemed to have a face mask hanging off one ear.

One rat turned to the other to ask a question.

"Do you think we should get the vaccine yet?"

"Definitely not. They're still testing it on humans," came the reply.

Reality Check

Fun fact 1: Around 4.5 million tons of food is thrown away by households in the UK every year, and most of it could have been eaten. That is enough to fill 38 million wheelie bins, or 90 Royal Albert Halls.
Fun fact 2: A million single use vapes are being thrown away every WEEK in the UK.

Several small spotlights positioned upon high poles, perforated the gloom of a mild moonlit November night. One of those lamps happened to illuminate a mound of stuffed black binbags which shimmered in the heady mix of LED and lunar luminescence. The only other light source was a small lamp which lit up the letters of a nearby sign which read Dedbury Recycle Centre.

On the topmost binbag sat two resting brown rats, each wearing surgical face masks. They both unhooked their masks from one ear at the same time, letting the masks dangle from their other ear.

"Remind me. Why are we wearing masks?" asked one of them.

"We need to be careful around those filthy humans. They carry some sort of deadly disease."

The removed masks revealed that one rat had grey whiskers and the other one white whiskers. Only the wear and tear on the fur of the grey whiskered rat hinted that it might be the slightly older one.

Above the rats, perched atop the highest spotlight, balanced a tawny owl taking keen interest in their activities.

Beneath the rats, almost every binbag had been ripped apart to create rat-sized holes, and many of the contents lay strewn about in random disorder. The two rats seemed oblivious to their recent work.

By and by, with one paw, White Whiskers scratched his bum enthusiastically until his face became the embodiment of bliss. Then, grabbing a dirty lump of cheese with the same paw, he bit into it and chewed contentedly whilst studying the ripped wreckage below him. He turned to address Grey Whiskers.

"Look at the mess you've made slashing your way into all these bags. Who do you think you are, Rat the Ripper?"

"You know what?" said White Whiskers, "I've been thinking about that."

"What?"

"About giving myself a name. I think if I call myself Rat the Ripper, I would gain respect."

Grey Whiskers stared at the older, and supposedly wiser, White Whiskers wide-eyed.

"Hmm, maybe, but naming yourself after a human mass murderer may not be the kind of respect you are looking for."

"Alright then, how about we name ourselves after those two humans we sneaked past earlier?"

"What were they called?"

"One called himself Albert and the other was called Clive. Who would you prefer to be?"

"I'll be Clive," said White Whiskers. "That Albert seemed a bit dim if you ask me. Okay with you … Albert?"

The older rat, seemed to have lost interest in the conversation, being too busy to respond. He was sucking enthusiastically on the teat of some small cylindrical metal device.

"Albert, what on earth are you doing?" asked the younger rat.

Albert exhaled a cloud of white vapour until the smoke completely surrounded Clive and set the creature coughing.

"Stop that. Stop. *Cough, cough.* Stop it, Albert. You know I hate that smoky stuff. And where did you find it anyway? The humans don't throw those things away. Not if they're still working."

As the smoke cleared, Albert curled his long tail around himself and smiled a contented smile.

"I found it on the ground. I think somebody dropped it. You should try it Clive."

Clive shook his head.

"You should be careful with things you find on the ground; they could be carrying diseases. It's hard enough concentrating on finding food here these days without filling your head with hallucinatory vapours. It just makes me nostalgic for times when food used to be plentiful." Clive coughed out some of said vapours, but inhaled enough to give him a whiff of wistfulness.

"Out of interest," said Albert, "where did you find your dirty lump of cheese?"

"On the ground. Under that bench outside the Centre," said Clive. "But I remember a time when there were rich pickings here. You never had to go looking under benches in the old days. Back then black bags were packed with still edible food. Those were happy times." He stared into the distance, wallowing in the dubious memory of some plentiful past.

"But now ... what annoys me is I know for a fact they throw away the same mountains of food as they ever did, and while us rats are standing by, willing and able to get rid of it for them, they don't send their waste food here anymore. Occasionally they throw you a morsel." He bit into the dirty cheese again, spat out a bit of gravel and pulled a face.

Albert nodded; a blissful, spaced-out look on his face. "I wonder where they send it all." He exhaled another cloud of smoke into Clive's face.

Clive tried, unsuccessfully, to blow away the vapour. "I have no idea. *Cough, cough*. I overheard one human say they send their waste food to a place called the Royal Albert Hall. Enough to fill 90 of them, apparently. But I don't know if that's true."

"Royal Albert," said Albert. "I like the sound of that."

"Anyway, if I knew for certain where they put it, I would not be here gnawing at this manky old lump of cheese. And that's another thing. Why can't we just have a home of our own? Wherever we go, we get pushed out. Not long ago everything was fine. The humans had something called 'lockdown'. We had the place to ourselves. Our lives improved dramatically. Then suddenly, it was over and we're back to our old life of skulking in corners and persecution."

Clive stared wistfully into the distance, thinking of those better times.

"You know what those humans do when their troubles get on top of them?"

"No. What?"

"They sing."

"Eh?"

"They sing. So that's what I'm going to do," said Clive.

"But you can't sing … can you?"

"I don't know. I've never tried. And if it's not good singing, I don't care."

"But what if I care?"

"I don't care about that either."

And with that, Clive filled his chest with air and gave it a go.

A Tip for Us

There's a tip for us
Some trash-filled skip for us
Some place filthy we can infest
Some place ... a pest ... can rest

There's a dump for us
We could make verminous
There's a home we can fabricate
Find a mate, procreate

Some dump
Somewhere
We'll find a new kind of challenge
We'll find a new way to scavenge
Somewhere

There are dumps for us
With cheesy lumps for us
Rancid and rank rotting food to spare
Much to share, don't despair

There's a dump for us
With dirt and detritus
Some may say that we spread disease
Carry fleas, spread faeces

Some dump
Somewhere
We'll live among their old shoppings
And decorate them with our droppings
Some dump, some tip
Somewhere ...

Clive expected some reaction, but none was forthcoming. Albert simply sucked away on his newly found teat, blowing smoke everywhere; a spaced-out expression on his face.

"Well?" said Clive. "*Cough, cough, cough.* Will you please stop that. I don't know why you like all that smoke. It's disgusting."

Albert thought about it. "I think the smoking is genetic."

"Genetic?" queried Clive.

"Yes. It was my granddad, Grampy Roland, first got our family into smoking you know. He worked in a lab."

"Your grandfather was a lab rat?"

"Yes. He really enjoyed the work. They let him smoke all day long. Actually provided free cigarettes for him. All day, every day. But what he loved most was the music. The lab piped in classical music. Grampy said they often played his favourite composer … Ratmaninov. But there was pop music too. He liked the Boomtown Rats."

"Who are the Boomtown Rats?"

Albert shrugged. "No idea, but apparently they didn't like Mondays."

"Who does? What happened to Grampy?"

"Sadly, he died young. Actually, he died twice. Both times from some kind of lung disease. It came as a complete shock to the whole family." Albert exhaled a white puffy cloud again.

Clive grabbed the end of his own tail with both paws and waved it around vigorously in front of his face in an effort to waft away the fumes. It didn't help. "Do you think that the smoking might just possibly have had something to do with his demise?"

"What a crazy idea. You know Clive, you can be very cynical sometimes."

At that moment, Clive was startled by rustling noises coming from the bottom of the heap of bags.

"What was that?"

"I can't see anything," said Albert, in his drug-induced stupor.

Clive scowled and raised his two front paws in front of Albert's snout. "How many paws am I holding up?"

"Seven," replied Albert. "Or none. Is it a trick question?"

"No use consulting you then." Clive looked down from his high position. A fox's tail bobbed between the binbags at the bottom of the heap. "It's a fox. We should get out of here."

"Why should we move?" said Albert, through his drug-induced bravado.

"I'll tell you why. Because we came here to *eat* food … not to *become* food!"

But Albert ignored him. The 'bravado virus' had infected his tail, his whiskers and everything in between. "I'm going down there to sort this fox out," he declared.

And with that, Albert scrambled down the pile, a flash of brown fur leaping from binbag to binbag until he came face to tail with the fox.

"This is our rubbish heap," he squeaked, feebly. Some of the drug effects evidently wearing off.

The fox turned to face him revealing sharp teeth and intimidating jaws, locked around the picked carcass of a chicken.

Albert bared his own teeth. Fortunately for him, the fox's jaws were otherwise engaged. It lifted its right front leg then raised its long middle claw and gesticulated with it in Albert's direction before moving on and disappearing into the night. Albert ran back up binbag mountain, exultant.

"What happened to the fox?" Asked Clive.

"It gave me the middle claw! But I dealt with it," he said, victoriously. "Foxes have no sway here. We are rats. Kings of the scavengers. We fear nothing."

Clive looked him up and down. "You idiot. You're lucky you are still alive."

Albert inhaled deeply again from the object Clive now considered to be the devil's device.

"Death means nothing to me."

"What are you talking about?"

"I'm saying that the fact that I am still alive is nothing to do with luck."

"I think that fox ran off with your brain."

"What I mean is I have no fear of death. Bring it on is what I say."

Clive looked at Albert pitifully. "That thing you are smoking has addled what was left of your mind. Everyone should fear death. That's how we survive longer. What makes you say you don't care?"

"Because I know about the afterlife," said Albert smugly.

"Then your brain is definitely addled. How can you possibly know about that?"

"Because my grandfather, Grampy Roland, went there once and returned to tell everyone about it. I told you. He died twice."

Clive gave Albert one of his hard stares. If not the hardest, then one of the hardest. Albert did not acknowledge it. He inhaled again from the smoking device.

"I have to assume it's the drugs making you talk this way."

"No, it's not," exhaled Albert. "Roland died one day while he was at work and went to heaven."

"If he died, then how did you find out about it?"

"Apparently there was a long queue to get in. They couldn't process everybody, so many got sent back. Roland was one of them."

Clive laughed. "You say there was a queue?"

Albert nodded.

"To get into heaven?"

Albert nodded again.

"Are you sure they weren't queueing to get into the Other Place? In my experience I have met many, many rats and very few of those are likely headed for heaven, if you know what I mean. The clue is in the name of our species. We are not referred to like Homo Sapiens, say, Ratto Sapiens. We are just rats. Rattus Rattus."

"I agree with you on that point," said Albert. "Humans don't seem to like us. Even though they rely on us to get rid of a lot of their food waste."

"Yes! That's what I'm saying. It's the humans who are messing up this planet. Not us. Who are the ones filling the oceans with plastic? Not us. Who is it has had to create enormous land fill sites to take all their trash? Not us. Who is it that pollutes the atmosphere with their cars and lorries? Not us. And who is it that defecates so much that it sometimes seeps into rivers and the environment? Not ..."

Clive stopped mid rant, distracted by the strained look on Albert's face. This look was followed by the emergence of a number of smelly black pellets being expelled from some unclear location beneath him and dropping down the side of the binbag.

He gave Albert a disgusted look. "Well, maybe that *is* us. But not just us."

Albert wiggled his bum as if to dislodge any remaining droppings and went back to his previous conversation as if nothing had happened.

"What happened to Grampy at that lab was all the humans' fault anyway."

"What? Him dying and going to heaven?"

"Yes. As you may know, heaven is divided into several sections based along geopolitical lines. All organised by humans of course."

"I did not know that. Enlighten me. Why is it that way?"

"Well, for example, say we rats were organising heaven, would we want to be living there with big predators like lions and tigers? Or even small predators like weasels and birds of prey."

Clive's whiskers seemed to shiver at the suggestion. "I suppose not."

"Humans are the same and many of them would rather have their own heaven than share one with somebody else. Unfortunately, heaven is managed by humans so we have no choice but to share theirs."

"How do you know all this?"

"I told you. Grampy Roland came back and explained it all. First thing he noticed while he was there was that there were many different entrance gates, each one for the dead of different nationalities. Mostly, people were just pushing forward and breaking through the gates into heaven. But Grampy found himself in front of the one gate where there was an orderly queue. The British gate. He said that originally, they would still have got in ... eventually, but the UK opted out of standard heaven in preference for one of their own, even though nearly half of them preferred the regular one. But with all the new regulations, everybody gets stopped at the gates and you get these huge queues. Anyway, he said there were too many to process that day and so a lot got sent back, including Grampy Roland."

Albert paused to take another huge drag on the smoke device. In the middle of doing so, he spotted a flash of tawny feathers cross the spotlight, heading silently toward them at high speed. Reflexively he exhaled enough of the white smoke to envelop both himself and Clive in time to confuse the owl, which screeched away into the night.

When the smoke cleared, an equally confused Clive saw a beatific-faced Albert, punch the air with his clenched paw.

"What just happened?"

"I saved us from an unsolicited dinner date with an owl. You're welcome. I told you. Foxes have no sway here. Owls have no sway here. We are rats. We are Kings of the scavengers. We fear nothing."

Albert inhaled again then wobbled a bit.

Clive took another bite out of his diminishing chunk of cheese. "I think you'll find it's the drugs that fear no one. Anyway, going back to your Grampy Roland and his crazy story … you need to explain to me this story about him 'coming back' from heaven?"

"It's not a story. It's all true. My dad was there as a young rat."

"In heaven?"

"No, of course not. My dad remembered the day very well. It was the same day Grampy told him they were being given some new kind of ciggies to smoke. The lab called them "Special" cigarettes. Out of the blue, my dad got a message from some of Grampy's co-workers at the lab later that day. They said Grampy had died. He went to collect the body. The lab owners had kindly put the body in a small cardboard box coffin and left it by the bins for convenience. So, so kind of them. They were wonderful employers. The coffin had obviously been supplied by the lab's doctor because the doctor's name was printed on the side."

"Really? The rats were provided with free medical care? What was the doctor's name?"

"Dr Martens. The name was printed on the box lid."

Clive nodded sagely. "Doc Martens, you say? Hmm."

"Anyway, dad accidentally dropped the box and Grampy came back from the dead."

"Or he just woke up from a drug induced coma," scoffed Clive.

Albert's face took on a pained expression. His whiskers drooped. "You don't believe me?"

"I'm just saying that there are often alternative explanations for the things we experience. By the way, how many other rats got sent back from heaven that day?"

"Only him.

"Really? Out of interest, what were his first words?"

"Apparently, he said, 'Those new cigarettes are really, really nice.' He was in a bit of a daze of course, him having just been dead."

Clive chewed the cheese for a moment. "Special cigarettes, you say? And then he told you he'd been to heaven?"

Albert nodded.

Clive shifted his gaze from Albert's glazed eyes to the metal smoking device stuck down his throat. He also nodded, but nodded to himself as Albert rising to his full height, raised both his front legs in the air and began jiggling his hips around as if to some unheard music.

"Stop that. Stop that right now before you do yourself an injury. You look like some crazed eastern belly dancer."

Albert's eyes lit up. "I am! That's exactly what I am!" He began bouncing his belly around. "Look at me. Don't you think I'm sexy?"

"I think you've lost your grip on reality is what I think."

Albert stopped for another drag and his expression completely changed from drug-related rapture to deep introspection. "Reality is an acquired taste these days, a mere optional extra, and I am happier without it."

While Albert waffled, Clive heard more rustling at the base of the binbags. The sound was getting nearer. As soon as he saw the source he screamed, "Cat!!!!"

Clive lunged at Albert and the two of them tumbled to the bottom of the heap, finally coming to rest under a pile of protective plastic.

The prone Albert raised himself on his elbows and rubbed his sore head.

"What happened?"

Clive gave him a long hard stare.

"We were attacked by an optional extra and I saved you."

"Thank you."

"You're welcome. What's that you were saying earlier? 'We are rats? Kings of the scavengers? We fear…?'"

"We fear nothing … except cats?"

Undue Influence

It was the end of the week and a warm summer morning at the Dedbury recycle centre. Albert and Clive were dragging a heavy old iron bedframe up the slope from the parking area for a disabled customer. Their final destination would be the metal waste skip but Albert was making heavy weather of it, grunting and sweating as they inched up the slope.

"Uh, uh, moan, oomph, whinge, mumble, mumble," he said. Or something similar. The exact noises he was making seemed to be either unspellable or unprintable. His hand scraped against a bit of sharp metal and his end of the bed fell on his boot.

"Ow!" he squealed.

Clive put his end of the bed down. "What's the matter with you today? You haven't stopped moaning since you arrived."

"It's alright for you. You're about 10 years younger than me. My old bones are trying to tell me something and I haven't been listening."

"We can stop here for a minute while I look for a Zimmer frame for you," joked Clive. "Maybe you should have chosen a different profession."

"Maybe," said Albert, puffing.

Clive was also happy to rest but did not say so. Instead, he said, "Here's a question. If you could meet your younger self, say, you as a teenager, what would you say to him?"

"I would say to him that if he ever thinks of a better job than working in recycling then jump at it. What about you?"

"I would say, 'Listen here young Clive, in 2010 you need to buy as much Bitcoin as you possibly can at around 10 cents per coin then sell in 2021 when the price reaches $68,000 per coin'. But in the absence of my could-have-been fortune, we need to shift this chunk of metal. Come on, let's get this old bed up to the top."

They continued up the slope till they got to the metal waste skip at which point the bed slipped from Albert's fingers again, this time coming down on his other boot.

"Ow!" he shouted. "Alright, that's it. I've had enough. I am going to put into practice the advice I just gave my younger self."

"What do you mean?"

"I've actually been thinking about a possible new direction for me and I am going to start right now."

He reached into his jacket and pulled out his phone and a tiny plastic tripod.

"I hope you are going to explain yourself otherwise I will assume the bed fell on your head rather than your foot," said Clive.

"I was watching YouTube recently and came across these videos of garden maintenance people who cut grass and tidy up gardens etc. What some of them do, is they do their normal paid work for 5 days of the week, but on the sixth day they roam around neighbourhoods looking for really overgrown messes of gardens. These usually belong to the elderly, the disabled or the financially strapped. Single mothers and the like. They find one of these and offer to mow and tidy for free. They set up a camera to film what they are doing and the amazing thing is that loads of people like to watch. I like to watch. It's uplifting seeing someone help others for free. And the even more amazing thing is that many of them earn even more from YouTube than they would get by doing one of their regular jobs. What do you think?"

Clive nodded, clearly impressed. "I agree, that's amazing. But what has that to do with you? You don't know anything about gardening."

"I didn't say that's what I was going to do. I am going to do the same thing, but film what we do here. There must be loads of people interested in seeing all their rubbish tidied away. And it might even earn me some money. And it might encourage more people to come here to recycle. I call that win, win, win."

Albert smiled at the perceived genius of his idea. He walked over to some old fridges a few yards from the main skips and set up his phone and tripod on one of them.

"I am going to start by filming us hefting this old bed in the skip and then I'll just leave it running for the rest of the day." He beamed at Clive and said, "Viewers will be hooked. I will start with YouTube then go on to TikTok and Instagram. I, my friend, am going to become a famous social media 'influencer'.

Clive laughed at the idea. "I don't think you want to associate yourself with influencers. I looked into it myself once and a lot of them are idiots." He pulled out his phone and began to search for an article he once read.

"I don't mind looking like an idiot as long as I'm a rich idiot," said Albert.

Clive did not appear to be listening while his fingers flicked around the screen.

"Ah," he said at last, "listen to this. They are talking about a few of them here. For example, this first one, a young female influencer, very popular until she started making some racist and hateful comments. When she started to lose all her followers, she tried to defend herself by saying 'I'm not a hateful person, I'm a Saggitarius'."

Albert shrugged. "So the lesson there is don't make any racist comments. Noted. Although I wasn't planning to do that anyway. And what's more, I can tell people at the start that I'm a Saggitarius so they will know I'm not hateful either."

"Alright," said Clive. "The next is from a very popular guy who said, 'I leave my fridge door open to combat climate change'. What would happen to the planet if we all left our fridge doors open?"

"Er, I assume you're thinking that's not actually going to reverse global warming?" said Albert, frowning. He pulled a scrap of paper from his pocket and wrote something on it.

"Noted," he said, without elaboration.

Clive decided that even if any elaboration was likely to follow, he did not wish to hear it. He continued by reading from the article.

"A 'healer' who calls herself Metaphysical Meagan on Instagram claimed that something which she calls 'perineum sunning', boosts energy, regulates hormones, and strengthens organs. She said aiming her bumhole at the sky for five minutes per day regulated her circadian rhythm and increased creativity. There was a short video of her doing a headstand on top of a hill at sunset. It went viral. This is the sort of thing you need to do to go viral, not filming people chucking beds into skips."

"I think I could do that," said Albert. "Was she wearing anything?"

"What?"

"Was she wearing anything? I mean … on her … posterior. Because if so, if she wasn't, I don't think I could compete with that. My naked posterior probably wouldn't have the same kind of draw as … you know …"

Clive was shaking his head and giving Albert his usual hard stare. "I wasn't suggesting you should upend yourself and wave your booty in the air, I'm just saying you need to do something like that."

"Oh," said Albert. "Well, I'm certainly not going to be waving anything else around in the air!". He went quiet for a minute then, "But did she? You know … I'm trying to imagine it."

Clive shrugged. "It's not clear in the photo they have here. But I assume so. Otherwise, how does one get the full hormonal and circadian experience after feeling the sun on one's perineum? Come on then, smile at the camera, grab the bed and heave-ho!"

And so, the old iron bed, after leaving an impression on both of Albert's feet, ended its limited life in this world and began its journey into everlasting life on the internet. And on the very same day, Albert's film of life at the Dedbury recycle centre took its place on YouTube alongside at least ten million short videos of funny cats.

* * *

And so it came to pass that when Albert arrived for the usual Monday morning staff meeting only three days after uploading his film, he enjoyed a round of applause from his fellow workers.

"What's going on?" he asked.

"You mean you don't know?" said Clive. "Have you not checked how many views your video has had?"

Albert shook his head. "No. My phone battery was dead and my charger conked out. I've not seen anything."

"I hate to admit it, but against my wildest expectations your video has gone viral! Over ten thousand views in just three days!"

Albert grinned from ear to ear. "I knew it! I should have done this years ago. I'll be rich. I'll be able to buy a new phone charger. Wait. I'll be able to give up my job! Heck, forget the phone charger. I could buy a private island in the Caribbean!"

Clive was now the one to shake his head. "I wouldn't get too excited," he said. "It looks like the video has been blocked and taken down for contravening YouTube rules."

"Why would they do that if the video was so popular? I don't understand."

"It was popular for a reason. And not a good one." Clive looked accusingly at Jabby.

"How was I to know you were going to be filming everything? You should have warned me," said Jabby, defensively.

"Let me read you the message from YouTube," said Clive. *"Sexually explicit content is not allowed on YouTube and is covered by our policies against nudity and sexual content."*

"What did you do?" said a shocked Albert.

Jabby refused to say, leaving Clive to explain. "It seems that the position of the camera covered all the skips, including the green waste one where Jabby sometimes ... erm, attends to the special needs of certain ladies ... and erm ... well, the camera caught some glimpses of ..."

"No!" exclaimed a shocked Albert. "You weren't!"

"It's a lie," asserted Jabby. "I was merely trying out something Clive was telling me about, so it's all his fault really."

"And what on Earth would that be?"

"Something called 'perineum sunning'. What you have to do is ..."

"I know exactly what you have to do", interrupted Albert, shaking his head. "But you had your trousers on, surely."

"Evidently not," said Clive. "While the video was still available YouTube statistics showed that the most watched parts were Jabby's bits."

* * *

By lunchtime, Albert had charged his phone using a charger in the office. He now sat with Clive on their bench opposite the centre, staring at his phone. He was still in a bit of a mood. His newly found career lay all around him in ruins.

"Don't look so down hearted," said Clive. "Maybe you'll be famous after all … for the shortest social media career ever? Maybe 3 days is a record of some sort."

But Albert wasn't listening. He was reading something on his phone.

"What are you doing?" asked Clive.

"Before they blocked my video there were some comments from viewers. I was just reading a few of them."

"Care to share?"

"Yes. These comments are cheering me up because Jabby is the 'butt' of their jokes and not me. Listen to these."

"I would like to vote for that guy by the green waste as 'Rear of the Year'."

"Some American guy says, 'It sure looks like British recycle centres get a bum deal.'"

"I've seen the front side of this recycle centre and never expected the backside would be so much more attractive."

"The end is in sight …"

"They should have renamed this video 'Rear Window'."

"At least you can see that this guy isn't doing a half-arsed job."

"And finally, one lady calling herself Miss Spank just left her phone number with the message, 'Call me'."

The Dedbury Falcon

"You look happy," said Albert to Clive, as he munched on his cheese sandwich.

Clive nodded, smiled and let out a contented sigh.

Albert was pleased to see it. The last week, he had not missed Clive's general grumpiness.

"Must have been a nice holiday then? Where was it you went? The Lake District?"

"Yes. It was terrible."

"The Lake District isn't that bad, is it?"

"It wasn't great. But I meant the holiday. You're lucky. You never have to suffer family holidays with your kids. Always having to GO somewhere or DO something. Listen, I wrote a poem about it. Want to hear it?"

"Not really."

"Well here it is anyway."

Wandering

I wandered only with a crowd
That drives en masse till Lakeland looms
When all at once I saw a cloud
Of traffic scented exhaust fumes
And trying to park beneath the trees
I ne'er saw queues as long as these

Continuing o'er hill and vale
That wondrous landscape to approve
To insignificance they pale
Compared with trippers on the move
Ten thousand saw I at a glance
Populate that vast expanse

Yet still `tis possible to climb
And lie beside some lonely tarn
To look on waters, stilling time
See distant sheep, low lying farm
And think how peaceful here it gets
Till wak'd by two low flying jets

For oft when from my car I gaze,
In roadside reverie myself to lose
In thinking of how many ways
There be to miss these endless queues
`Tis then I think, `tis good to roam
But better still to stay at home

"So you see I'm just happy to be back here in the peace and quiet, where nothing ever happens."

Albert put on his 'I know something you don't know' face when Clive said this. Clive picked up on it.

"What? Something did happen? Have I missed something?"

Albert continued with his knowing look but said nothing.

"You're not going to tell me? Alright then, let me guess. Bogsy lost his glove puppet? Ms Hunter demonstrated a new yoga position? Jabby had another one of his 'Adventures'?"

Albert shook his head at all these suggestions. "No. You'll never believe it."

"How could I if you don't tell me?"

Albert's expression morphed into conspiratorial as he leaned into Clive's side of the bench and whispered, "A woman arrived here on the first Monday you were away, late morning, after the weekly staff meeting."

"What?! A woman?" exclaimed Clive, feigning shock. "How extraordinary. I'll not be able to live with myself having missed that!"

"You can be sarcastic if you like but this was like no woman I have ever met."

"Other than Victoria and your mother, how many women have you met?"

"You may mock, but wait till I explain what happened. This woman turned up and walked right up to me. I was working up at general waste …"

"I'm all ears. Why don't you start from the beginning?"

Albert cast his mind back and tried his best to recall every detail.

"It began as a normal day. A day like any other. People were rolling up in their cars and relieving themselves."

A look from Clive prompted Albert to elaborate. "Relieving themselves of their old junk. I'm there watching them. Making sure they don't put their stuff in the wrong skips. You know, the usual thing, when this woman walks up. She's not in a car, she just walks up. She's not carrying any trash with her. And believe me, the catsuit she was wearing was so tight there was nowhere to hide a tissue, never mind a binbag."

"Catsuit? You'd better describe what she looked like in more detail."

"I'd say early twenties. She was tall, taller than me, nice hair. Black. Her figure was er, well packed, like a … like a … well, like something that's well packed."

"Is that the best description you can do? Hmm. Did Jabby see her?"

"Yes."

"How did he describe her?"

"Jabby said she had long, midnight black, wavy hair, so wavy you could swim in it. He said he could imagine diving into it on some warm summer evening by some moonlit forest glade and then …"

"Stop!" interrupted Clive. "I don't need that level of detail. What else did he say about her appearance?"

"He said she had a smile wider than superfast broadband and it made him just as happy."

Albert's thoughts wandered at this point and his head was now firmly back in that moment, one week earlier, as he began to tell Clive the story.

* * *

"Well, hello there handsome," said the good-looking young woman in the catsuit. "I think you are just the man I've been looking for."

Albert swivelled his head to see who stood behind him, but there was no one.

She stood right in front of him now. "Yes, I'm looking at you. What do you call yourself?"

"Al-Al Albert," said Albert.

The woman smiled a wide, knee-trembling smile. "Pleased to meet you, Al-Al Albert. Look, I have found myself in a really awkward situation and I am looking for a white knight to save me."

She almost pinned him to the side of the general waste skip with the strength of the pleading in her eyes. "Do you think you could be my white knight, Albert?"

Albert nodded. "What can I do for you?"

"I am so glad you asked that." The woman's face now became all sad. "You see, Albie, my poor mother …" She looked skyward. "… God rest her soul, died recently and an over enthusiastic home clearance company accidentally removed a certain item of the greatest sentimental value that belonged to her."

"I have of course been in touch with the removal company and they absolutely assure me that all items of any kind of reusability were brought here. So you see Albie, I am entirely in your hands."

"Wh-wh what was it exactly that you are looking for?"

"Well, here's the thing Albie. It should be very easy to find. What I am looking for is a large luggage trunk. You couldn't miss it if you saw it. Brown leather with a checkerboard design."

She paused a moment. "Let me be absolutely honest with you Albie."

In Albert's mind, when somebody says 'Let me be honest with you', you can be pretty sure they will not be telling the whole truth. And if they say 'Let me be absolutely honest with you', the next words to leave their lips are almost certainly going to be an outright lie. Clive had taught him this. However, he was still surprised when she put her luscious lips close to his ear and spoke in a whisper.

"My mother is in the trunk."

Albert took a startled step backwards, in shock. She grabbed his arm and fixed her wide, reassuring smile on him.

"I mean to say that the trunk contains my mother's ashes."

Albert relaxed. He considered the stated size of the trunk and was about to say, 'Your mother was a big woman then', but thought better of it. She continued.

"Do you think that's something you might have seen?" She gave Albert a penetrating stare. Much harder than the hard stares Clive was in the habit of giving him.

Albert shook his head. The cat-woman looked immensely disappointed.

"But I can have a look for you."

Cat-woman, now suddenly all smile, squeezed Albert's arm. "I knew you were the man I was looking for. Here, take my card. And Albie, if you, or any of your people can find it for me, you will be well rewarded." She stroked him with her smile again. "And I will give £50 to the finder. Oh, and by the way, if anyone else comes looking for the trunk, especially someone calling himself 'The Falcon', don't trust him. He is a very dangerous individual. You do not want to cross The Falcon. If you see him, be sure to call me immediately."

And with that, she padded back down the slope to the exit, Albert watching her, every step of the way.

* * *

Clive listened to all this with disbelief. "So, who was this woman?" he asked.

In his head, Albert was still watching the cat-woman.

"Hello! Earth to Albert!"

"What?"

"I said who was she? What … was … her … name? She gave you a card."

Albert emerged from his reverie.

"Lush," he said. "Miss Veronica Lush. She was trouble. As it turns out."

"Did you find her trunk?"

"I can't tell you that."

"What? Why not?"

"It's for your own protection. The less you know, the better."

Clive gave Albert one of his standard hard stares. "I think you need to explain."

Once again Albert's thoughts went back to the previous Monday …

* * *

That evening, as Albert was about to lock the entrance gate and go home, a shiny, black limousine turned into the gate entrance and stopped in front of him, its headlights causing him to squint.

The driver, a mountain of a man, wearing a black uniform, got out and approached Albert. He was tall, about six three and chunky with it. The sort of chunkiness that comes from working out at the gym every day and from eating industrial quantities of protein. Protein laced with substances that would get an Olympic athlete banned. His nose was slightly squashed and pushed to one side. Albert got the impression that the man facing him may be a practitioner of the headbutt school of diplomacy.

"Sorry. We're closed," said Albert.

The man mountain ignored him. "Are you Albert?" he said, the act of speech exposing the fact that one of his teeth was missing.

"Who wants to know?"

"My employer wishes to talk to you."

"And who might that be?"

"You may call him The Falcon."

Albert shivered at the name, after the stark warning from Miss Lush.

"I am not going anywhere," he said, as confidently as he could.

Man Mountain was not impressed. "Hand me your phone."

He said this in a way that made Albert feel it would be beneficial to his health if he complied immediately. He handed over his mobile.

"Log in code?" demanded The Mountain. Albert told him.

"Why do you want my phone?" asked Albert, hesitantly.

"Just checking you are on WhatsApp." The Mountain moved his thick fingers around the screen for a minute. While he was doing this, Albert braved a question.

"Why is he called The Falcon?"

"He likes old black and white crime movies. He sees himself as the thing everyone is looking for."

The Mountain finished with the phone and handed it back to Albert.

"The Falcon will speak to you now."

Albert was about to repeat that he was not going anywhere, when a previously unseen passenger stepped out of the limo and into the headlights to stand next to The Mountain. Albert saw that this was a much smaller individual, about five foot tall. Pale and spotty-faced, and to his surprise …

"But you're just a kid," he said. "You don't look more than twelve!"

The Falcon raised his own mobile and tapped the screen. Albert's phone pinged. It seemed that The Mountain had created a WhatsApp group for himself and Falcon. A message awaited.

"Actually, I am fourteen, almost fifteen. And I have acne to prove it. Laughing with crying eyes emoji. I am pleased to meet you, Albert. My personal assistant, Cecil, tells me you do a lot of texting."

"Some," said Albert.

The Falcon frowned. Cecil pointed to Albert's phone and grunted. "The Falcon only communicates by text. Use WhatsApp for your responses."

"Wait," said Albert, when he opened WhatsApp. "This WhatsApp group includes somebody called Eyas. Who's Eyas?"

"Eyas is Falcon's younger brother. If you're wondering, eyas is the word for a young hawk or falcon. Google it."

Albert repeated his previous verbal reply, this time by text. "I wouldn't say I do a lot of texting, but some. Do you have a disability that prevents you from talking?"

Every time Falcon replied there was a short delay, as if the response was coming from the moon.

There was a ping. "No. I am merely a product of my generation. Happy face emoji."

"But surely you use your voice sometimes?" texted Albert.

Cecil answered this. "There is only one word Falcon will say out loud."

And, before Albert could enquire as to the identity of that word, Falcon shouted it at Cecil. "Pimple!"

This prompted Cecil to move in close to Falcon's face, examine it, find the offending zit, and squeeze the life out of it. He then took a small pack of antiseptic wipes from his uniform pocket and used the next wipe available to remove the remnants of blood and pus from Falcon's face. Falcon then continued texting as if nothing had happened.

Albert's phone pinged again. "If you are uncomfortable with my method of communication then you should be happy you are not facing my younger brother. He can only communicate using emojis."

"Emojis?!" Textclaimed Albert.

Ping! "Yes. What can I say? The youth of today! Rolling eyes emoji." Falcon rolled his eyes to mimic his emoji as Albert read the rest of the text. "No offense but old people like you sometimes struggle with texting. It seems that texting does not appear to make you uncomfortable, so may I assume that you are a man who likes to text?"

"I'm not old, I'm only 45! But I am happy to text," texted Albert.

Ping! "That's good Albert, old man, because I also like to text. And I will tell you that I am a man who likes to text with a man who likes to text. Happy face emoji."

Falcon smiled each time he texted back a happy face emoji. And each time he smiled, Albert noticed that some of the many spots on Falcon's cheeks moved around in a disturbing manner. It was as if some spots were imitating the expansion of the universe while others were falling into the black hole that was his mouth. Although, as his mouth had no need to open, this was a poor analogy.

"What shall we text about?" texted Albert.

Ping! "Excellent! You are a man who texts right to the point. I just know we will get along. First of all, I need to know if you are the official representative of Miss Lush in terms of negotiation for the erm, item of interest."

"And what item would that be?" texted Albert, coolly.

Falcon's response to this took a little longer even though his thumbs danced at great speed across the screen of his phone.

Ping! "Come, come, Albert, that is not the way we negotiate. No, no, no. Let me put my emojis on the table. I am prepared to triple the amount of money offered by Miss Lush. That is, if the item in question is readily available and in its original, unopened condition. Smiley face emoji with halo."

Albert saw an opportunity, grinned and set about texting. "In that case, Miss Lush offered me £200 for the item in question."

Ping! "Crying laughing emoji. £200 does not begin to approach the true value of this object."

"Shocked emoji," texted Albert. "What? For an old suitcase?"

Ping. "This is not any old suitcase. It is the Louis Vuitton checkered Damier pattern trunk. Link to web page. PS Damier is French for checkerboard. Smiley emoji."

Albert followed the link and read the following: -

At the start of the 20th century, tourism was the domain of the wealthy who could afford ocean liner voyages—not forgetting the hired manpower needed to lug around giant steamer trunks. Luggage during this time was a serious status symbol, and no brand was more coveted than Louis Vuitton. This trunk dates to the early 1900s when the luxury manufacturer introduced its now iconic checkered Damier pattern. VALUE: £20000.

Albert's phone pinged again. "This particular one was owned by Ingrid Bergman and used by her during the making of the film Casablanca. Believe me, this particular example is worth much more than £20000."

It pinged again. "I think £600 would be a suitable offer for your services. For that I expect you to relinquish your ties to Miss Lush and work exclusively for myself. The trunk must be pristine and unopened. The contents must not be disturbed in any way. Do I have your agreement?"

Albert nodded then texted, "What if I don't find it?"

Ping! "Then I might have to speak to you using my voice. Three angry emojis."

"Should I be scared?"

Suddenly Falcon shouted at his assistant again.

"Pimple!"

Cecil put his face directly in front of Falcon's, spotted the offending pimple and brutally squashed it between his fat fingers. A wet wipe followed, to clear the blood. Cecil casually tossed it in the road. They both got back in the limo and drove away.

Albert stood there, not quite knowing what had just happened until his phone pinged again some 30 seconds later.

"Don't be a pimple. WhatsApp me when you find the trunk. You have two days."

* * *

Clive's head was spinning. "I can't believe I missed all this. What happened next? Did you find the trunk? Are you £600 the richer?"

Albert sat there silently. His head still reliving the strange events of the previous week.

"Well?" urged Clive. "Are you going to tell me or do you only communicate through WhatsApp now?"

He poured some tea from his flask into a plastic cup and gulped it down like it had whisky in it.

"I'll have to tell you the story in order. As it happened."

Albert's eyes glazed over. Clive could see that his head was back in last week again.

* * *

The following day, a police car drove into the recycle centre and parked. Out of the car stepped Detective Inspector Wubble and her assistant. Albert knew Inspector Wubble from previous encounters, particularly the time when there were problems with the centre's previous manager, Bossy McBossFace. Albert watched from his position at general waste as they walked over to the office. A couple of minutes later they emerged and set off toward him. The forty-five-year-old Inspector puffed a little coming up the slope. She had the body of a woman so frustrated by her job that she had arrested far too many chocolate biscuits in an effort to retain her sanity. More revealing was that it appeared none of those biscuits had ever been released from jail. Every one of them had been executed. Two minutes later he was face to face with her.

"We meet again." she said. "Don't panic. I am not about to arrest you for having a body in the boot of your car this time, or even for that awful facial hair. I am hoping you may be able to help us with our enquiries."

Albert put his hand over the stubble on his face as if to protect it.

"That was *not* a body," he asserted.

"No. But that shop mannequin looked so much like one, maybe I should have arrested you for wasting police time."

Albert's mind raced around for some crime he may have inadvertently committed and not remembered. He couldn't help himself. Whenever he saw the police, he always felt guilty of something, but he could think of nothing that might be prosecutable. As a general rule, he felt that the major part of his life was usually so boring that he didn't consider the police would be remotely interested in any of it. He relaxed slightly.

"How can I help you?" he said.

"We have been closely following the activities of a certain individual who goes around calling himself The Falcon."

Albert gulped.

She reached for her phone and showed him a photo of a too familiar, spotty-faced lad. When Albert did not immediately admit acquaintance, she expanded the image so much that only a part of Falcon's face and five fiery red zits that looked about to burst, filled the screen. She kept the image a few inches from him until the recent memory of burst pimples made Albert recoil.

"Alright, alright, I admit it. I have met him."

"So why were you reluctant to tell me?"

"Because I have met him."

"I know what you mean," said the Inspector, putting her phone away. "He gives me the creeps too. Anyway, I'm glad you admitted meeting because we knew he had been here."

"How? And if you knew he'd been here, why ask me?"

"As to the how, you do not need to know. But why I asked? I just enjoy winding you up. It's one of the few joys left to me in this wretched job of mine. Now then, let me save us all a lot of time. We know Falcon came here and we know he came looking for some kind of old trunk. Do you have it? I should tell you we are more interested in the contents than in the trunk itself."

"Falcon told me not to open it if I found it."

"Ah, thank you Albert. Now that I know you have communicated with him, I know you must be in a WhatsApp group with him. So, here's what I want you to do."

This conversation was not going the way Albert expected. Wubble seemed far too skilled at getting information from him. He wanted to upset her flow.

"Wait a second. How do you know I haven't already found the trunk and passed it on to Falcon?"

"Because, my dear Albert, if you had found that trunk you would have called the police immediately." She said, smiling.

"Why? How can you possibly know what I would do?"

"Because that pimple-pocked friend of yours is a drug dealer. The elusive trunk is packed full of grade A drugs and had you found such a trove of illegal trauma, you being the upstanding citizen I know you to be, you would have called us. Am I right?"

Albert nodded.

"Now. If an item such as the one we are looking for was ever brought here, what would have happened to it?"

Albert scratched his police-offending stubble for a moment. "Anything reusable would have been put into the shipping container for the benefit of the public or for charities to collect."

"Show me."

Albert led the police officers down to the container.

"Suitcases and such are near the back."

They wandered through a mess of old bikes, chairs, and any kind of household goods you could imagine before reaching a pile of battered suitcases.

"Some of these look so dilapidated surely no one would want them," said the Inspector.

"You'd be surprised. Old luggage often does well on Bargain Hunt. Generally, the more worn the better." There was a largish trunk on a table next to a suitcase.

"That trunk looks about the right size. Open it."

Albert knew it was not the trunk. Wrong colour, dark blue for a start, not the checkerboard design Falcon was looking for. He said nothing and pressed the latches. The trunk lid released and he lifted it to reveal … emptiness.

The Inspector stared at the two items on the table with a look of disappointment, at which point her assistant spoke for the first time.

"Looks like an open and shut case, Guv."

Wubble gave him a withering look. "Officer Kuff, if you ever make a comment like that again you will be back on traffic duty."

"Hee, hee, hee, I thought it was quite funny," giggled Albert.

Wubble marched out of the shipping container and headed back to the car. Albert and Officer Kuff followed.

"I have a question," said Albert. "If this Falcon lad is such an evil drug dealer, who is he selling to?"

The Inspector took a small mirror from her handbag and used it to adjust her hair. "We had an appeal from the headmaster of one of our local schools who told us the incidence of hard drugs found amongst pupils had increased significantly over the last 6 months. When we checked with other schools, they all told the same story. We asked around the school ..."

Albert looked surprised.

"... No, we did not ask pupils to tell us who the drug dealer was. We asked who they thought the richest kid was. They said the boy who gets dropped off in a limo. We asked when did that start happening. They said about 6 months ago. We've had our eye on him ever since but haven't been able to catch him in the act."

She paused, allowing time for Albert to take it all in. "Now. Here's what I want you to do. Tomorrow morning at 9am you WhatsApp him to say you have the trunk. When he gets here, tell him it's at the back of the shipping container. We will hide in there lying in wait."

"But what happens when he sees we haven't got the trunk?"

"Not a problem. All we want is his phone."

"His phone? How will that help?"

The Inspector looked at Albert as if he was stupid. "Really? Somebody who communicates only by text? Everything they ever texted will be on it. Every deal they ever did, plus a list of all his connections."

Upon which, the two police officers got in the car and drove away.

* * *

Throughout his recollection Albert had been taking the occasional sip of tea. He stopped talking to take another swig but it had all gone. Clive quickly grabbed his own flask and poured some of it into Albert's cup.

"Go on. You can't stop there."

Albert recognised that this was one rare occasion when Clive was hanging on his every word. He would milk the moment. He took his mind back to last Wednesday morning.

* * *

At 9am precisely, Albert opened WhatsApp and sent his message. "Trunk found. Could be what you are looking for. It's locked and feels heavy."

It was not long before a familiar black limo appeared in the recycling centre car park. Albert noticed it straight away. It was hard not to. He watched as Cecil opened the door for his master and Falcon emerged, phone in hand. Wubble and Officer Kuff had arrived earlier in an unmarked car. They were hiding in the shipping container.

It was less than a minute before Albert's phone pinged.

"Where are you?"

"Come to the shipping container."

Ping! "Cecil will with be with you first, to prepare the site."

"Prepare the site?"

Ping! "I do not like surprises."

Before you could say 'controlled substance', Cecil passed Albert by, ignoring him completely, and stepped inside the container. One elderly lady, browsing some old picture frames was grabbed by the elbow and summarily marched out.

"Sorry, we're closed," said Cecil. He scanned the container and seeing no other browsers, got out his phone and typed a single word into WhatsApp. Albert was able to see over Cecil's shoulder that the word was, "Clear!"

Falcon then emerged from the limo and walked over to join them. The three men walked through to the back of the container to the suitcases. Albert had covered the blue trunk with a cloth in order to disguise the ruse until the last minute. As he removed the cloth, Wubble and Kuff emerged from their hiding place.

The two police officers moved forward. Inspector Wubble said, "Are you the despicable toerag, familiarly known as Falcon?"

Falcon turned around. He looked so surprised that even the pimples on his face seemed to jump.

"I see that you are," said the Inspector. "You are under arrest."

Falcon put on his angry emoji face and looked to Cecil for help, but Officer Kuff had moved in next to him.

Inspector Wubble read Falcon his rights. He made no acknowledgement, other than by a change of expression from angry emoji to shocked emoji, in every way acting as if he did not understand what was going on.

Albert handed the Inspector his phone and she understood instantly. She opened WhatsApp and wrote two words. Falcon's phone pinged.

"You're nicked!" Read the message. Her next message read, "Now do you understand? Rolling on the floor laughing emoji."

Ping! "I've done nothing wrong," texted back Falcon. "You can't arrest me for looking at suitcases."

The Inspector was enjoying being in charge of Albert's phone.

"I am arresting you for drug dealing. We have you on video passing drugs to one of your dealers at St. Lukes school."

Ping! "Who told you where I'd be? Was it him?" Falcon pointed at Albert as if to underline his text.

"No. It was an anonymous tip off."

Ping! "Who? Two angry emojis."

"Do you not know what the word anonymous means? Maybe you should spend more time *in* education instead of disrupting it. Smiley face emoji."

Albert looked on nervously, watching intently through all this as Falcon's head appeared to reach boiling point. His face gradually began to exhibit a uniform ruddiness such that it was no longer possible to differentiate his zits from the rest of his face. That was until two of the zits, now engorged with blood, looked like they were about to erupt. Albert, guessing what might come next, took a step back just before Falcon shrieked, "Pimple!"

Cecil attempted to spring into his usual pimple-popping action, but was held back by officer Kuff.

"Sorry sir, but you are also under arrest. For possible collusion."

At this point, a police siren was heard and a squad car pulled into the recycle centre. Moments later two more policemen appeared and the two suspects were taken away. Before being handcuffed, Cecil was able to pass Falcon a couple of wipes, which he used to clean up his face.

As he was being led away, Inspector Wubble took Falcon's phone.

"I'll take that. This will be used in evidence. It will confirm intention to supply drugs or maybe even who you actually sold them to."

She turned to Albert. "Thanks for your help. We will be in touch if we need a statement from you."

* * *

"Amazing," said Clive. "So, was that the end of it?"

"I thought so but no. The next day I got another visit from Miss Lush. She grabbed me as I was leaving."

"Where?"

"In the office. It happened like this …"

* * *

Albert stopped in his tracks when he saw Miss Lush walking toward him. He was locking up for the night. She wore a catsuit similar to the one she wore last time, except that this one seemed even more figure hugging.

She sidled up to him, slid her hand under his open hi-vis jacket and began to closely examine the fabric of his shirt. She looked lovingly at the shirt, like she desperately wanted to try it on, while he was still wearing it. Albert's face reddened.

"I came to thank you in person Albie."

"Thank me?"

"For dealing with my brother."

"Your brother?"

"Are you just going to stand there and repeat everything I say?"

"Everything you say?"

"Yes. You are still doing it." She removed her hand from his chest and took a step backward.

Albert tried to pull himself together. "Do I know your brother?"

"Of course. My brother, Falcon."

"Falcon is you brother!?"

"Yes. Well, half-brother anyway. We have the same mother."

"So why are you thanking me."

"Because you managed to get him put away."

"That wasn't me. The police had an anonymous tip off."

Miss Lush smiled her disarming smile and almost purred. "That was me. I sent the police incriminating video evidence and put them onto his meeting with you. It all went far better than I hoped."

"Why would you rat on your own brother?"

"I don't like him. He's an obnoxious pimple who can drown in his own pus for all I care."

Albert was shocked. "That's the kind of sisterly love you don't hear every day."

"You don't want to know what he did to me." She paused lost in thought for a moment. "But I'm going to tell you anyway.

When our mother died, he got my stepfather to make me go out delivering drugs. Girls are often chosen to run and deal drugs because they are less likely to get caught than boys and are usually treated more leniently by the courts. Also, women don't get noticed as much if they are hanging around schools. I was doing that for the last year until my stepfather was caught and sent down a month ago. That was when I first tried sending anonymous messages to the police."

At this point she grinned a Machiavellian grin.

"The trunk was one of the places Falcon stored his stock-in-trade. So, I arranged for it to be delivered here to spite my step-brother."

Something had been worrying Albert and it was still making him tense. He had to ask the question.

"Your mother's ashes weren't really in that trunk, were they?"

Miss Lush smiled at him again. "I suspected you would see right through me. No, of course not."

Albert visibly relaxed.

"The bag of white powder in the trunk was cocaine."

Albert immediately tensed up again.

"Cocaine?!"

"Yes, enough to get him put away for up to seven years for possession alone. That's if I could get him caught with it. Unfortunately, that didn't work out … did it, Albie? The trunk seems to have disappeared. I don't suppose you would know anything about that?" She laid a penetrating stare on him.

He ignored the question. "What are you going to do now?"

To his surprise, she leaned over and kissed him on both cheeks.

"Why, I'm going to take over my brother's drugs empire, of course."

And with that, she slinked away, Albert watching, open-mouthed.

* * *

"And that's it?" queried Clive. "Is that the end of the story?"

"Yes, more or less. Except ..."

"Except?"

"Except that on Friday Ms Hunter received a letter from the police commending me for my brave actions. Said I was a community-minded citizen helping them take down a violent gang leader. She was so pleased about it she gathered us all in a mini-meeting to tell everyone."

Clive was bemused. "And what's wrong with that?"

"Well, I would put the emphasis on the 'violent gang leader' bit. I played a part in Falcon's downfall. I don't want anyone to know about it. I want to keep a low profile. Don't want to be on the radar of a criminal drugs cartel. What if they come for me?"

"You mean as in 'bump you off', 'eliminate you', facilitate your journey to the great recycle centre in the sky etc?"

Albert nodded.

"Well at least you will die in the knowledge that you did your duty as a citizen. And I promise I will say some kind words at your funeral." Clive was grinning but Albert was not.

"Somehow that does not give me the reassurance I need."

Clive could tell Albert was agitated about it. He relented. "The Falcon is in jail now, along with his henchman. You can relax. What do you need to worry about?"

"He won't be in jail. Too young. They'll put him in a Young Offender's Institution. Not secure enough if you ask me."

At that moment Albert's phone pinged.

"It's a message for the Falcon WhatsApp group! It's from his brother Eyas."

"What does it say?"

"It doesn't 'say' anything. Falcon said Eyas only communicates by emoji."

"Show me."

Albert, ashen faced, turned the screen to face Clive. The message contained three emojis, all skulls.

"You better start writing my funeral speech soon," he said.

* * *

That weekend, Albert sat opposite his Aunt Lucy in the lounge of her house, located some 500 metres from the recycle centre. Between them stood a large trunk with checkerboard pattern. Upon this rested a tea tray with a teapot, two cups of tea, a bowl of sugar and a plate of biscuits.

Albert took a bite out of a chocolate biscuit and sipped his tea.

Aunt Lucy's dog Prince lay content at his feet.

"I see you've made good use of the trunk you found at the recycle centre," he said.

"Oh yes. It's wonderful. All of Prince's toys, bed, blanket, leads, dog dishes etc. fit in there nicely. The place is so tidy now. Thank you so much for bringing it over for me. You know, I've shown it off to all my friends and relatives. They are all so envious. They all want to know where I got it."

"And do you tell them?" asked Albert nervously.

"Of course. I tell everyone about the reuse section where you work and of course I mention your name every time."

Albert suddenly felt a little sick. He put down the rest of his biscuit.

"Erm, when you opened the trunk, did you find anything in it?"

"Now you mention it, there was this plastic bag full of white powder."

"Erm, and what did you do with it?"

"Funny you should ask. When I opened it, Prince took one whiff and started to go barking mad. He was so wild I had to get rid of it in the end."

Albert relaxed a little. At least that won't come back to bite me, he thought.

"Erm, when you say 'got rid of', what do you mean exactly?"

"Well, it looked like flour or something so I threw it in a food waste bag and chucked it with the recycling." She laughed. "It'll probably be back with you Monday morning."

The blood drained from Albert's face and he groaned inwardly.

Managing Expectations

As the staff gathered in the office for a special meeting, Ms Hunter was on top of her desk. As usual she was practicing yoga positions. Currently she had her hands down on one end of the desk, feet at the other and her nether region up in the air forming a perfect triangle with the desk.

"Welcome to the meeting boys. They call this position adho mukha svanasana, more commonly known as the "Downward Dog". They say this exercise strengthens the whole body and calms the mind. I find it particularly good for toning the gluteus maximus."

Albert whispered to Clive. "Who's Gluteus Maximus? Sounds like some Roman Emperor."

"It's your bum," whispered back Clive.

Ms Hunter twisted her head to look at her audience and ask, "What do you all think? Should I keep this position or try another?"

"Maximus!" shouted Jabby.

"Maximus!" echoed Bogsy and Ted.

Within a few seconds they were all chanting, "Maximus! Maximus! Maximus!" while Ms Hunter maintained her perfect triangle.

The chanting continued even when someone knocked on the office door. Albert went to see who was there and opened it to a young gangly lad whom Albert assessed to be in his late teens.

"Hello. I am your new member of staff," said the lad.

"Er, really?" said a bemused Albert. "Er, you better come in."

Albert brought the lad to the front where Ms Hunter remained in her Downward Dog, the men still chanting, "Maximus! Maximus! Maximus!"

Albert had to clear his throat loudly to get everybody's attention.

"Ahem. We have a visitor."

Ms Hunter collapsed her triangle in one smooth movement, ending up sat on the front edge of the desk facing the newcomer.

"Of course. You must be Ben. Welcome." She leaned forward to shake his hand. She turned to the audience.

"Listen everybody, this is Ben, our latest member of staff. He is a school leaver so be gentle with him."

She turned back to Ben. "Do you do yoga by any chance?"

"No," said Ben in a downbeat tone. "I've never done any kind of exercise."

"What are you doing here then?" laughed Clive.

"My mother suggested it. She's a climate activist. Wants to save the world. She said I should get a job that's green and … useful."

"What are you doing here then?" repeated Clive.

"Never mind him, you're here anyway," said Ms Hunter. "We'll sort you out with some protective clothing later but for now, I have an important message for everybody from head office. I've read it and it's all about finances. They are saying that money is so tight they want every department to think of ways to either save money or to make more. You may have heard on the news that at least one big council has just gone bankrupt. There have been others and there may be more. So, if anybody has any ideas, let me know and I will put them forward. Any ideas?"

"Maybe we could charge for conducted tours of the facility. Rent the premises for special interest groups," said Ted.

"Like who?" said Clive. "Who would want to come here?"

"I don't know. We could advertise."

"Didn't we have the Dedbury Walkers Group stop here once?" suggested Albert.

"Wait a minute," said Clive. If we have all these groups coming here, they will need toilet facilities. All we have is our two staff toilets. We already get pensioners asking to use our toilets all the time. All since they closed the public toilets in town to save money. It's getting ridiculous. And half of them don't even ask. The other day I had to get in a queue so long I almost had to go behind a skip. And I would have if another staff member hadn't beaten me to it."

"Really Clive," said Ms Hunter. "It can't be that bad."

"It is," said Albert. "You know things are bad when Clive starts writing about it. Do your limerick Clive."

Clive shrugged. "If you like. But it's an old one. I'm sure you've heard it before. However, I think it sums up the situation: -

When dumping, there are one or two who
Like to use the same loo me and you do
Now some would say this
*Was **taking** the piss*
*But they always **leave** pee-pee ...*

                                        ... *or doo-doo*."

Ms Hunter put on an expression of exaggerated pity.

"Aw, poor you. If you get really desperate Clive, I'll let you use the ladies toilet."

"Really?"

"Yes. Only for pee-pee though. It's a no-no on the doo-doo. Anyway, I think you should be more caring toward pensioners. You may be one yourself one day. I should tell everyone that a new aspiration has been added to the

Council's mission statement and that is to promote a more caring society and well, I actually agree with them on this one. They say we should encourage people to help each other. If we had a more caring society, there would be fewer problems in the world. From now on, our motto should be, 'Who Cares, Wins'."

While she was speaking, Albert sniggered and whispered to Clive, "That's very similar to your own personal motto, isn't it?"

"You mean, 'Who Cares?' Yes it is!"

Ms Hunter continued, "Look, I'll advertise on local forums for potential interest groups who might want to use our premises. If we get any responses, Albert can decide who we allow."

"Why Albert?" said Clive.

"Because I will be on holiday next week," she grinned. "And as Albert is most senior, he can stand in. Oh, and by the way, due to a glitch with mid-week skip replacement, they are all being changed over the long weekend instead. So, we will be closed Saturday, Sunday and on the Bank Holiday Monday. I hope you all enjoy your weekend."

Just then, to Ms Hunter's surprise, a skip delivery truck arrived at the gates.

"Jabby, go and investigate. They shouldn't be dropping any new skips until the old ones have gone." She turned to Albert and Clive. "In the meantime, I want you two to look after Ben. Show him the ropes. Now, if everyone is good, I'll get on with sending an email to head office about our money saving idea and put a message on the local community forum."

A few minutes later, Jabby returned to the office to report back.

"The driver said the skip is on his list for delivery. He can't take it back. I told him to drop it on the spare ground behind the office. It's not one of our usual massive skips, it's a domestic one so it won't take up too much room. He can come back for it next week."

* * *

"Come with us," said Clive to young Ben when the meeting was over. "We'll get you the obligatory high-vis jacket."

While he was putting it on, Clive was curious about something Ben had said earlier.

"Was that true about you not doing any exercise, or were you joking?"

"It's true."

"So, do you actually know what exercise is Ben?"

"Is there an app for it?"

Clive looked shocked.

"That was a joke," said Ben, with no hint of playfulness in his voice or expression. "Of course, I've heard of exercise. It's just that until now I have not had a need for it. Look, I am fully prepared to pull my weight here. How effective I will be is open to doubt at this point. But I need a favour. Can you let me do something 'green' so I have something positive to report back to my mother?"

Clive and Albert looked at each other. "We'll show you the work," said Clive, but we'll leave it you to decide how green and useful it is. Some of it must be useful, surely, won't it Albert?"

Albert nodded, unconvincingly.

"And if not, then … how are your lying skills?"

"About as good as my exercise skills," said Ben gloomily. "Whatever happens, I have to impress my mother somehow."

Clive observed that Ben looked almost suicidal when speaking of his mother.

"Ben, we do recycling here. The definition of an environmentally friendly job if you ask me. Your mother is bound to be impressed with that."

"I doubt the recycling here will meet her high standards." Ben said, despondently.

"Surely she can't be that bad."

"You have no idea. Whatever happens, I have to keep this job. I need this time away from her or I'll lose my sanity."

* * *

The following Tuesday, after the bank holiday weekend, Albert stood in front of Ms Hunter's desk, excited to take the weekly meeting. All weekend he'd been practising what to say. His managerial ability would shine through. All problems would melt before him. Staff would give glowing reports to Ms Hunter. He visualised his career launching towards a rose-tinted future … until rudely awoken from his fantasy.

"Why don't you show us your Downward Dog, Albert?" shouted Jabby.

"Please don't," said Clive. "And before you start, the coffee machine is broken. What are you going to do about that? You know I can't function without my morning coffee."

"How should I know? What do we usually do?"

Jabby answered the question. "We usually find another old coffee machine from the electrical waste. But we don't need to do that this time. The rest of us all have coffees. Really good ones."

Jabby, Ted and Bogsy all held up their coffees. They were not drinking from their usual mugs, but from commercial-looking cardboard coffee cups with the words 'Café Joe' printed on them.

"Here," said Jabby, taking two coffees from a tray on the chair next to him, "Joe made coffees for you and Clive too." He passed them over.

"Joe?" said Albert. "Who's Joe?"

"Our barista. He calls himself Cappuccino Joe."

"Our barista? What are you talking about? Has a new coffee shop opened in town?" He sipped the coffee. "Oh, that's good. How did you manage to keep it warm?"

"Erm, the café is really not far from here."

"How far?"

"Erm, well, just behind us."

"Jabby, why are you being so evasive?"

"Erm, well, you remember the skip they sent us in error on Friday?"

"Yes."

"Well, that's the coffee shop. Joe runs it from the skip."

Albert was extremely confused. He turned around. Through the dirty back window of the office, he could see the vague outlines of the skip. It appeared to have been adapted in some way.

"What makes this Joe think he can just wander in here and sell coffee to us whenever he pleases?"

"Oh, he doesn't wander in here, he lives here. And he doesn't sell us coffee, he gives it to us for free."

"Wait. He lives here? What are you talking about?"

"He lives in the skip," said Jabby, as if it was the most natural thing in the world.

Jabby was talking about the extraordinary in terms that made it sound like a complete stranger living in a skip in a recycle centre was completely normal. Albert could not cope with this at the moment. He had an important meeting to conduct.

"He lives in one of our skips!! He's a squatter?! Why didn't you just tell him to bog off?"

"It's complicated," said Jabby.

Albert put his head in his hands and shook it. "I can't be dealing with this squatter right now. I have the weekly meeting to do. I'll look into it later."

He glanced at some pieces of paper he was holding and made a conscious effort to calm down. When he was ready, he squared up to his audience and cleared his throat.

"Ahem. Wait. Where's young Ben?"

"Outside," said Jabby, "he had to call his mother."

"Well, I need to get on with this so I'm going to start." He cleared his throat again.

"Ahem. First thing on the agenda is the email responses to Ms Hunter's advert for groups who might be interested in paying to use our premises on off days. I've printed them out. I'll read them.

The first one is: -

The Dracula Club – Apparently, they have been banned from most of their usual meeting places."

"Where's that?" asked Clive.

"Local church graveyards, mostly. They meet only at night. They like to lie on top of old graves and surprise passers-by. They are looking for alternative locations that would offer a similar, quote, 'ambience of creepiness' including a heightened sense of threat. They say they are always looking for new members. Especially female members. They have a slogan. 'Join our Fang Club'.

Next is the Dedbury Green Party. They hold meetings, explain the principles of recycling, and ditch some of their junk at the same time. They say they usually have speakers who for past meetings have spoken on various ecological issues ranging from food waste to plastic pollution. They hope that someone on our staff will give a talk on similar environmental issues. They point out that they are still looking for speakers on Ozone Layer Depletion or Loss of Biodiversity. Their slogan is 'Be green. Be very green'."

Clive interposed. "Apart from that sounding vaguely threatening, I think we can safely discount that one, don't you? Nobody here could do that." said Clive.

"Not so fast," piped up Ben, having come back inside to hear the end part of Albert's speech. "If I heard you right you need a speaker on green issues. I could find someone to talk about all those things and at the same time you would be doing me a favour."

"Really? Who?"

"My mother. She never shuts up about all that kind of stuff."

Clive nodded to show he understood. "We'll make a note of that. Hmm. Any others Albert?"

"Yes, one last group. The Dedbury Naturist and Antique Collectors Club. Apparently, they er, 'Like to gather once a month to show off their er, junk and er, valuables to each other'. They also like to refer to themselves as 'The buff with their stuff'.

"I might join that one," said Jabby. "I'm buff."

"Yeah, but you have no stuff," said Clive.

"So that's it," said Albert. "I was thinking about inviting the chairmen or chairwomen of each of these organisations. They all said they would need to check our premises to see if they are suitable for their needs. It would be great if we can have them all. They will all pay us a fee. Ms Hunter will get the kudos and the Council will have the income."

Clive shook his head in bemusement. "You mean invite all of them? Even the naturists? I think naturists are dangerous."

"Dangerous? That's crazy. Of course we want to invite everybody. Naturist's money is as good as anyone else's."

"On your head be it. Is that the end of the meeting?" said Clive.

"No. There's one more thing I'd like to say. Listen up everybody. We're a team and as such let's keep this show on the road. We need to make sure we all sing from the same hymn sheet and get all our ducks in a row. If anyone has any more ideas, they should touch base offline so we can cross-pollinate and any good ones we can run up the flagpole and see who salutes."

Clive gave him a hard stare and took him to one side to have a quiet word.

"What on earth are you talking about?" he whispered.

"I looked online for popular phrases a manager would use to his staff."

"Popular phrases? Popular with managers maybe, not with staff. Keep on like that and you'll be managing a riot."

"Oh. But Ms Hunter always says something inspiring. I don't know what to say. What kind of things do staff like to hear?"

"They like to hear things like, 'Let's finish early' and 'You are all getting a pay rise'. However, for now, why not just say 'Any questions? If not let's get on with it'."

Abert turned back to his audience. "Any questions? If not let's get on with it."

"I have a question."

"Yes Ted?"

"Where is this flagpole you were talking about?"

"Just get back to work everyone," said Albert.

* * *

The next morning, Albert sat at Ms Hunter's desk. Finally, he was in the big chair. Now he could show he was management material. Fortunately, the chair wasn't too big. He wouldn't fall foul of Clive's low opinion of managerial chair culture where top managers measured the size of their status, or whatever, by the size of their chair. 'The bigger the chair, the bigger the plonker', Clive would say. Well, he was going to show everybody that he was not a plonker and this small chair was a good start. He would meet the three candidates one by one, agree deals, please Ms Hunter and bring in a pile of money for the Council. After that, who knows?

Right now though, the first of three potential candidates for use of the recycle centre sat facing him. It was hard to ignore the man sitting opposite. He wore a black suit and a high-collared cape lined with blood-red coloured silk for a start. Not to mention his slicked-back, black hair. And the fangs of course. The fangs were very hard to ignore. He cut a notable figure when Albert showed him around the site before ending back in the office.

Albert had been a little nervous about this first meeting from the start. He never liked horror films or horror stories. Dracula, ugh! He had brought with him to the meeting, a kind of talisman, just in case. It was in the left-hand pocket of his jacket. He gripped it tightly as he spoke.

"So, Mr erm, Draco, what do you think? Will you be using us for your meetings?"

Draco removed his fangs and placed them on the desk before replying. "Call me Vlad," he said. "Sorry about the fangs. It's kind of expected of me. Makes it so hard to talk though."

Albert was not sure how to respond. "I'm surprised you came here ... during daylight hours, I mean."

"Ah, I had to come now because my work is mainly night shifts. But as to the use of your premises, I do not think it is what we are looking for. Ideally, we are after an element of danger, unease. Either to create it or experience it. I do not see any of that here. Do you have anything here that might give one a sense of ... foreboding?"

Albert considered. "Maybe a bit of old asbestos. That plus the habits of one or two staff members. Otherwise, all I can think of is rats. We do have rats."

Vlad pulled a face, showing he was mildly impressed. "At least that's something. I'll mention it to my members. Sadly, I do not think it will sway them. After all, we could bring our own rats to add to the ambience. Maybe you have bats? Bats would be an advantage. Bats are so hard to get hold of these days, don't you think?"

"Er, I'm sure you're right. But we don't have bats … as far as I know."

"You would know if you had them. Wonderful creatures. Did you know, bats are one of the main pollinators of bananas? No bats, no bananas. Vampire bats are particularly interesting. They can drink half their body weight in blood." He looked into the distance and licked his lips.

"But I digress. No, the main problem with this place is that there will be no opportunity for chance encounters with the public. For example, when our group turns out near the blood donor's unit, that usually gets a reaction. Then there's graveyards of course."

Albert tensed at the mention of graveyards. Graveyards also made him uneasy. He gripped the talisman in his pocket more tightly. Vlad spotted the movement and gave Albert the evil eye.

"You know, all the time I was talking, you seemed nervous. Had your hand in your pocket, fiddling with something. What is it? Show me. On second thoughts please don't. I don't want to see anything disgusting. You know, I thank you for your time, but no. We will not be using your services."

"No, no, no," said Albert, not wanting to lose the business, "it's not what you think." He removed the talisman from his pocket, revealing it to be a large clove of garlic."

"What? That's even worse. I am affronted. Goodbye!"

Upon which, Vlad rose and with an angry and dramatic swirl of his cape, headed for the door.

Albert called to him as he was leaving. "Excuse me. Haven't you forgotten something?" He tipped his head at the desktop.

Vlad swirled around again, walked back to the desk, picked up his fangs, inserted them and left.

* * *

A couple of minutes later Albert was up at general waste, his elbows resting on the lip of a skip, looking down at the car park. He stood next to Clive who was doing the same thing. They both watched Vlad attempt to extract his cloak, which was trapped in his car door.

"Ted says he recognised the guy," said Clive. "His real name is Willy Johnson. Ted says he works for Tesco's, stacking shelves after hours. Not so impressive when you know that, is he?" said Clive. "Anyway, how did it go?"

"Not great. I didn't think it was our kind of thing. No environmental connections. Head office would never have approved. I managed to get rid of him."

"How?"

Albert removed the garlic from his pocket and put it to Clive's nose.

He recoiled. "Really? I thought that only worked in stories."

"Just call me Vampire Hunter," said Albert.

"Who's next?"

"The Green Party. They will be here tomorrow morning."

* * *

For the second time, Albert sat behind Ms Hunter's desk. This time opposite a smartly dressed woman of about his own age. In green trouser suit and matching emerald-coloured shoes and handbag, she looked the part. He was resolved to do better today but had not expected the demeanour of the Green Party representative to be more intimidating than that of Vlad Draco. He was thinking if Vlad drank her blood, she would probably have sucked the blood back. Or at the very least, eaten him for breakfast. He attempted to sweeten her.

"May I offer a warm welcome to an esteemed representative of the Green Party … Mrs …" He glanced down at his notes. "Mrs Woods."

"You may call me Fern," was her stern reply.

"Fern Woods. What an appropriate name for someone concerned about the environment," said Albert, still attempting to sweeten her.

If the woman across the desk from him had a standard facial expression, Albert rated it as, 'stoney' and it did not change following his comment.

"We are not the Green Party. We are the Greener Party. A completely different organisation."

"I apologise. Must've been a typo," he said, squinting at a copy of her email, which indeed said Greener Party on closer examination.

"We, at the Greener Party, believe that the Green Party are nowhere green enough. I mean, the Green Party want us to get to carbon net zero. What a joke. We advocate going carbon negative. Our slogan is," and at this point her voice deepened and sounded vaguely threatening, "'Be green. Be very green, and …"

"So I've heard," interrupted Albert. "That sounds a little intimidating, if you don't mind me saying so."

"Do not interrupt me. As I was saying, our slogan is, 'Be green. Be very green … and then be greener'. If we are going to save our planet, intimidation is probably not enough. We need to wake people up. However, I concede that some people do say some of our policies are a little intimidating."

"Oh? What policies are those?" asked Albert, instantly regretting the question.

"There's litter for a start. We would put litter wardens on every street and give them the power to give on the spot fines. Second offence and you go to jail … or worse."

"Worse?"

She made the all-familiar gesture of slicing her fingertips across her throat.

"Then there's water pollution. We say that a director of any company polluting rivers should be made to drink only that water until it's cleaned up."

"And what if they won't?"

She repeated her fingertips across throat gesture.

Albert gulped. "And you say some people find these policies intimidating? I can't imagine why. Erm, Mrs Woods …"

"I told you. Call me Fern!" she barked. Her stern face quickly melting into a less than sincere smile. "Being on first name terms is so much more friendly, don't you think?"

"Erm, Fern, do you think your organisation will be using our premises?"

"That depends. We are always on the lookout for speakers on topics of environmental interest and we would expect you to provide someone."

"Ah," said Albert, thinking he had an instant solution to this, "although no one on our staff is qualified in that respect, we know of someone who would be ideal. She is the mother of one of our new employees."

"Would that be Ben?"

"Er, yes," said Albert, surprised, "you know Ben?"

"Of course I do. I am Ben's mother." She stood, saying, "That would be no good at all. I'm sorry but if you have no intelligent speakers then we shall be going elsewhere. My message to you sir is we should all start taking the environment much more seriously if we are to save this planet, otherwise do you know what is likely to happen?"

Albert imitated her fingers across throat gesture and threw her a quizzical look.

"Exactly," she said. "Goodbye."

* * *

A few minutes later, Albert was up with Clive by general waste watching Mrs Woods get into her car and leave.

"You can come out of hiding now Ben. Your mother's leaving," said Clive. "You know, I don't think someone who comes here in their car can be all that green. I mean, why didn't she get a bus and walk?"

"Electric car," said Ben.

"Oh," said Clive, deflated because his attempted character assassination had been foiled. He turned to Albert.

"Did you convince her to use our place for their meetings then?"

"No. Her terms were too onerous. And she hid the fact that she was Ben's mum. I told her to get on her bike."

"Never mind, you still have one more group to talk to tomorrow. The Naturists. At least they won't be hiding anything."

* * *

The woman sitting across the desk from Albert the next day was, he guessed, a few years younger than himself. She unclipped her voluminous ginger hair to let it tumble over her shoulders, front and back.

"Do you find it warm in here?" she asked, flapping her hand in front of her face like a fan.

"Shall I open a window?" said Albert.

"No no, I'll just take my cardigan off."

The representative of the Naturists and Antique Collectors Club removed her cardigan and placed it on the back of her chair. Albert could now see that her hair fell to just below her shoulders.

"So, Mrs ... Cox ..."

"That's Cox, C-O-X, in case you were wondering," she grinned. "But call me Joy."

"So, Joy, you've had the tour. What do you think? Is this somewhere of interest to your group? Our rates are very reasonable."

She traced the V of her blouse's neckline with her fingers. "You have certainly got me interested, Albert. You don't mind me calling you Albert, do you?"

Albert shook his head. She looked him up and down and leaned forward in her chair.

"You look like a fine figure of a man Albert. Have you ever considered becoming a naturist yourself?"

He shook his head again and could not help blushing.

"You really should. You wouldn't believe the feeling of freedom it gives you. And as a member of our group, I promise you would never get bored. We like to refer to ourselves as, 'Mad, Bad and Unclad'."

Albert began to think that Joy was actually more menacing than Vlad and Fern combined. He was beginning to feel rather warm himself.

"Erm, I think it was me supposed to be recruiting you. Not the other way around."

Joy leaned back in her chair again. She cast her eyes around the office and pulled a face.

"Well, to be honest, it wasn't what I was expecting. This office is very boring. The outside areas are interesting though. I can imagine members being active in and around the skips."

"What? You want to do your naturism thing outside?!" Albert was shocked.

"Yes. Of course."

"Where people could see you?"

"Yes."

"Well, I don't think … I mean … it's not …" Albert was struggling to find a reason why he could not allow them outside.

"Yes?"

"Excuse me a moment. I just need to check something." He stepped outside and called Clive to explain his dilemma. A few moments later he stepped back in, now in a much happier frame of mind.

"I am sorry to inform you Joy, but we would not be able to allow your members outside. It is a question of Health and Safety you see. We have strict rules here about dress and the fact is, strong boots and hi-vis jackets must be worn at all times out there."

"Oh dear," said Joy, "that would not do for our members, not at all. How disappointing. Perhaps I could persuade you to overlook that little rule for us?"

"I don't think so."

She began fanning her face with her hand again. "You know I am still so warm. I wonder what I can do to cool myself down? Oh, I know …"

She began unbuttoning her blouse.

"STOP!" shouted Albert. "I told you there are health and safety issues. Our liability insurance does not cover accidents whilst naked."

At this point Joy gave up, buttoned her blouse and put her cardigan back on. She stood up, more in a huff than in the buff, and headed to the door. Before leaving, she turned around to make one last comment.

"See if I care. If you don't want our business, we can always try the sewage works."

* * *

Albert walked slowly up to general waste for the third time that week, where Clive listened to his report. It was clear to Clive that Albert was depressed about having to lose the naturist's business.

"You have a face like a wet sock," he said.

"Maybe. But that observation is not helping."

Clive made an attempt to lighten his mood.

"I still think nudists are dangerous," said Clive. "We're better off without them."

"And why would that be?" asked Albert, glumly.

"I read somewhere about this massive cruise ship that almost capsized as it sailed past a nudist colony in the Med. Apparently, a thousand passengers suddenly ran to one side of the ship to look and it almost keeled over."

The story did not elicit even a flicker of a smile. Albert still felt very down. As though his head was under a dark, heavy cloud. Worse than that. The cloud completely enveloped him. All three potential new sources of income had come to nothing. He would have no good news to tell Ms Hunter. His chance as stand-in manager had been a complete failure.

He explained how he was feeling to Clive.

"Oh well," said Clive. "At least things can't get any worse. Anyway, there's another reason why having all those naturists around would be a bad idea."

"Oh?"

"There would be so many flagpoles around that nobody would know which one to salute."

* * *

It was Friday morning and Albert's final job as manager would be to give the squatter his marching orders. He had been putting this moment off as he usually avoided conflict wherever possible. But in this case, he had no choice. If he had any shred of a chance to impress Ms Hunter then the squatter must be evicted. He and Clive wandered around to the back of the office where Cappuccino Joe's skip house and café stood on some spare ground. The flared ends of the skip had been built out with pieces of wood to provide extra height and a curved roof put on top. Everything appeared to have been cobbled together from bits and pieces salvaged from recycling. There was even a small window in the side made from a piece of double-glazing.

Clive moved to the window and tapped on it. It opened and Joe popped his head out.

"Good morning, Clive. Can I get you anything? Your usual?"

This prompted Albert to give Clive a hard stare for a change.

"Your usual?"

Clive ignored him. "Yes, please Joe. Your Cappuccino Special with cinnamon sprinkles. You should try one Albert. Make that two Joe. And do you mind if we have a word with you?"

Joe had found a couple of old plastic tables and a variety of chairs in the skips. They were set out in front of his café. He brought the coffees and sat with them.

"How can I help you?" he said.

"This is Albert," said Clive. "He's the one in charge."

"I am so pleased to finally meet you, Albert. I have heard so much about you. What do you think of the coffee?"

Albert did not usually drink coffee but he took a sip and his eyes lit up.

"This is wonderful! I've never tasted coffee like this before. But look, I'm sorry, but I can't let you stay here. There are rules. What are you doing here in the first place?"

"I used to work at a coffee place in town. The business was building up nicely for the owner but with lockdown it began to struggle. He kept it going as long as he could but two weeks ago, he had to close it. He had to let me go. I could no longer afford to pay my rent and got chucked out. I was desperate and saw this place was closed. Managed to get in on Friday night and saw the empty skip. I fixed it up over the next three days. I'm pretty handy at DIY and saw I could get practically everything I wanted from the recycling. Your staff helped me with some things too. I can't thank them enough."

"Helped you?"

"Yes. The best thing was the mattress from Jabby. Said he gave me his best one. Does he collect them or something? Come over and look inside."

The three of them walked over to the skip house and Joe opened the window so they could see inside. Albert was astonished to see it was beautifully fitted out with shelves, work top and even a kitchen sink. There was a kind of mezzanine raised area where Jabby's mattress made what looked like a comfortable bed. There were even pictures on the wall and a potted plant.

"And you found all this stuff in the recycling? I have to admit you have done an amazing job with it. But I'm sorry. There are so many reasons why I can't let you stay."

"Like what?" said Clive.

"Like the cost of keeping the skip here for a start."

"Joe has agreed with the skip company to pay them £50 a month rent on it for the foreseeable future."

"Oh. Well, what about basic services. I mean, how will Joe even wash himself?"

"I am a member of the local gym club. I go there and take a shower every day," said Joe.

"Well, what about cooking?"

"I have a very small portable camping stove. Not good for cooking much other than food from cans but it will do me for now. If someone brings an old functioning microwave for recycling that would be an improvement."

Until now it seemed that Joe had an answer for everything. "Ah," said Albert, "but where would you get your electricity?"

"He gets it from our outdoor supply." Clive pointed to the electric cable running from the back of the office and into the skip.

"We can't afford to let you use our power," said Abert.

"That's why I'm selling coffee. Here …" Joe took some cash from his pocket and handed £50 to Albert. "This is for my electricity and for my rent. I was hoping to give you more but I'm still building the business."

"Fifty pounds from selling coffee. But I thought you were giving it away free."

"Only to you and your staff. I charge regular prices to your customers. The regulars even tip me."

"You have regulars?"

Albert could not believe that finding a reason to evict Joe would be so difficult. But he really needed to find one before Ms Hunter got back or he would be in bigger trouble than he already was. A final thought occurred to him. Even Clive would agree with him on this one.

"But what about toilet facilities. You don't have a toilet in there."

Clive answered this. "We gave Joe a spare key to the office so he could use the toilet whenever. And he can get water from our outside tap."

"Really!" said Albert. "After all your whingeing and limericks about pee-pee and doo-doo? Why?"

"Free coffee," said Clive, smiling.

Albert shook his head. "No. I'm sorry. No. You'll have to move out before Ms Hunter gets back and that's my final word."

He walked away.

* * *

The following Monday, Albert outlined to Ms Hunter how he had failed to recruit a single society. He was as glum as could be throughout his entire confession.

"Cheer up Albert," said Ms Hunter. "You did well. Being manager may not have worked out for you, but you have been a good leader."

"What's the difference?"

"Management is about doing things right. Following the rules etc. Anyone can follow rules. They just have to be pig-headed. Leadership is about doing the right thing. Even if that means not achieving your goals. That requires courage. But you're too hard on yourself Albert. A little birdie told me that you still managed to pull victory from defeat."

"I have?"

"Yes. You managed to recruit Cappuccino Joe."

"I did?"

"Yes. And for several reasons, that's worked out far better than I could have imagined. Remember, the Council are trying to promote a more caring society. We are helping someone who would have been homeless otherwise, saving them money. Then there's the income they wanted. Joe is covering the cost of his skip rental plus extra for being allowed to stay here. Everything the council wanted."

"Plus, the coffee is amazing," chipped in Jabby."

"Plus, the coffee is free," squeaked Bogsy.

"Plus, the cups are recyclable. Nobody has to do the washing up," grinned Ted.

"Plus," said Clive, "I just checked and our ratings on TripAdvisor have gone through the roof over the last few days. Customers are raving about the coffee and describing us as a destination. Other than money, nothing pleases the council more than high approval ratings."

Just then, Joe walked in with a tray of fresh coffees.

"Wonderful," said Ms Hunter, "I would like to propose a toast. Everybody please raise your coffees to Manager of the Week, Albert."

"To Albert!"

More Lies, More Damned Lies and not much Recycling

The quality of the weekly Monday morning staff meeting had improved immensely since the introduction of Cappuccino Joe's delectable coffee. The staff sat around relaxing and chatting while Ms Hunter performed improbable yoga routines on her desk. Joe had just delivered their coffees and hung around when he saw what Ms Hunter was doing.

"Mind if I join you?" he asked.

She unravelled herself and smiled at him. "That would be wonderful," she said. "This lot never seem to want to join in. They have no idea how healthy a bit of yoga can be. Have you ever done any yoga yourself?"

"Try me," said Joe. "What about some two person positions? How about we start with the double downward dog?"

Ms Hunter was now beaming. "Do you want to be on top or would you prefer if I were on top?"

Suddenly, their conversation had taken a turn that caught the attention of the rest of the staff. They stopped talking among themselves and turned to the front. Clearly, they were keen to know who would be on top and to see what would happen next.

"I like being on top," said Joe, kicking off his shoes.

Ms Hunter morphed herself into her now familiar downward dog, her orange dungaree-clad rear uppermost. Despite the limited space on the office desk, Joe managed to put his hands on the desktop a little way in front of her then, one leg at a time, manoeuvred each leg to rest in the small of her back, his own rear now at a slightly higher elevation than hers. The end result had an acrobatic quality which impressed the onlookers so much they broke into a spontaneous round of applause.

After a few minutes, Albert observed the desktop duo to be enjoying themselves so much that Ms Hunter seemed to have forgotten she was supposed to be holding a meeting.

"Ahem!" he coughed.

At this, the duo disengaged and disentangled themselves.

"I really enjoyed that," said a flushed Ms Hunter.

"Me too," said Joe. "Maybe we could do it again sometime."

"Yes. I'd love to go downward dogging with you. In fact, I can't wait."

"I would invite you to my place, but it's a bit small."

"I'm sure something could be arranged. I'll give you my number."

Her eyes stayed with Joe as he walked to the door and left. Albert cleared his throat again.

"Oh, yes, the meeting. Erm, are there any issues to raise? If not then let's not waste time and get on with our jobs." She glanced around the room not expecting any response but to her surprise Ben, their new school leaver, raised his hand.

"You're not at school any more Ben. You don't have to put your hand up here."

"I do at home," he said.

"What is it, Ben?"

"I have a confession to make."

Ms Hunter gave him a sideways look. "We are helping to save the planet here Ben, saving people's souls is someone else's job."

"I know. But this is very much in the saving the planet category."

"Alright then. Say what you have to say."

Ben reached into the pocket of his hi-vis jacket and held out a small, black plastic object on the palm of his hand. The object was smaller than a packet of cigarettes but larger than a vape.

"I have no idea what that is. You will have to enlighten us."

"This, Ms Hunter, is a GPS tracking device. My mother told me to put it in an item of waste so she can track it."

"What? Without asking? And why?"

"She is trying to prove that not all the recycling here gets recycled. She suspects that the recycling world is lying to us and it all ends up in landfill anyway. She didn't want me to ask you because she thinks people here might be involved in the conspiracy."

"So, why did you decide to tell us?"

"Because that would be deceitful. I don't want to begin this new job with a lie. I don't want to become like my mother. She's well intentioned, but she lies all the time and expects everyone else does the same."

"Your mother lies all the time? Why?" queried Clive.

"Well, she's a politician. Need I say more?"

"Probably not." Clive turned to Ms Hunter. "What are we going to do about this?"

She thought for a moment, then appeared to make a decision.

"I think we should go ahead and put the device in the waste. I would like to know what happens to our waste as much as anyone. Ben, how does your mother track the device?"

"She has an app. You can track its progress on your phone."

"Can we all download this app?"

"Yes. I'll send you the link."

"Alight then. I propose we all download the app and review the tracker's progress next week. Agreed?"

The pool of nodding heads in front of her indicated everyone was of the same mind.

"If there are no more issues then let's get on."

Ben's hand went up again but slowly descended when he remembered he did not have to do that.

"Sorry," he said. "Habit. There's one more thing I need to say. My mother must never know that you all know. Okay?"

"You mean we should lie to her if she asks?" said Clive.

"Yes. Absolutely. You should lie."

* * *

Lunchtime that day, Albert and Clive sat ... not on their usual bench, but shockingly, on plastic chairs at one of half a dozen tables laid out in front of Joe's café. Albert was not entirely happy about it.

"Somehow, I feel disloyal to our bench. That bench has been our friend for many years. One sniff of a cappuccino and we've abandoned it. I feel dirty."

Joe came over and placed two fresh coffees on their table. Albert put his nose to his coffee and breathed in deeply.

"On the other hand, there's no harm in a little variety." He opened his lunch box and took out a cheese sandwich.

"So, what did you think of our doggers?" said Clive.

"I thought they were both a bit touchy-feely. I'm surprised Ms Hunter let him get away with it. What do you think?"

"I think there are an awful lot of lies flying around right now."

"Yeah. It's not right. I was very disappointed in Ms Hunter when she agreed to deceiving Ben's mother. I've met her and she's not a woman I would like to cross ... ever."

Clive shrugged. "I wouldn't worry about it. People lie all the time."

"What do you mean? I don't lie. If I did, I would have to confess it. And I hate having to admit to it when I go to confession."

"You could always lie in confession," grinned Clive. "No. I mean there are many, many lies in this world so common that most people hardly notice them."

"Such as?"

"Well, there are personal lies like, 'Thanks, it's just what I've always wanted'. Or 'I would never lie to you'. You can guarantee if someone says that to you, they will be lying through their teeth. And then there are lies married people say to each other like, 'I only had one beer'. Or, 'It didn't cost that much'. Or 'You look great in that …' whatever.

Then there are the lies you get from business. Like, 'People are our most important asset'. In reality, people are their most worrisome and unpredictable asset. Their most important assets are really their financial assets. It would not surprise me at all that, if someone did a study into it, they would discover the average giant corporation would rank the value of their paperclips higher than their staff.

The other business lie I hate is when your manager says, 'We judge people by their performance'. What they mean is 'I judge your performance based on how much I like you'. Oh, and this is my favourite, 'The customer comes first'. What they mean is, 'I come first'. They will take care of customers when it benefits them and ignore customers when they can get away with it. Nobody ever says 'I come first', or 'The shareholders come first', which is what's usually going on."

"I'm sorry I mentioned the subject," said Albert, but Clive had not quite finished his rant.

"Then there are the lies we tell our children. What parent hasn't said to their kid, 'If you don't go to sleep, Santa won't come'? Or, 'Yes, we're nearly there'. Or, 'When the ice cream van's music is on, it means there's no ice cream left'. And if you want to really bring parent lies up to date, what about this I heard one of the mothers say at my kid's playgroup, 'There's an app on my phone that tells me if you really brushed your teeth or not'. And don't let me start on the lies we tell ourselves."

"I won't, I won't," said Albert, thinking Clive's rant had stopped this time. He was wrong.

"And the thing that's annoying me most right now is call centre recorded messages. 'Your call is important to us'. Ha! And, 'We are currently experiencing a high number of calls'. Two of the biggest lies ever! Why is it that when I call any big organisation it is always the same message? Why has nobody ever just answered the phone? If your call was really important, why don't they f …" At this point Clive noticed Ben was coming over to sit with them. He changed what he was about to say.

"Why don't they flipping well get some extra staff in?"

Ben put his coffee on the table and sat down. "You were about to say a swear word then, weren't you?" said Ben.

"No." said Clive, defensively.

"And now you just lied. Everyone tells me how to behave, but acts completely differently. How will I ever know what's true?"

"That's not possible," said Clive. "Like someone once said, and it's worth repeating, there's no such thing as truth. The truth is just a lie that hasn't been found out."

"How did you become so cynical?"

"He was born like that," said Albert.

"I got like this by working," said Clive. "But don't let me depress you. You are too young to be depressed … yet. Enjoy a little optimism about life while you can."

"You seem to have forgotten about my mother."

"Oh, yes. And selective forgetting. That also helps."

Ben put the tracking device on the table.

"We need to put this with some waste. Ms Hunter says we can decide which."

Albert and Clive exchanged blank looks.

"We have no idea," said Clive. "I think you are best qualified for that. What with all the er, indoctrination, I mean, education you have had from your mother on this subject."

"You were right the first time. The word indoctrination does not come close to describing the experience. But if she were here, she would say any kind of plastic waste. Millions of tons of waste plastic from British businesses and homes are ending up in landfill sites both here and across the world. The expectation is that the huge amounts of waste being sent overseas will be recycled and turned into new products abroad. However, that is not always the case. We may as well track some of ours to see where it ends up. Hopefully we will find that it all goes to legitimate recycling plants in the UK. If not, and mother gets to hear of it …"

"What?" said Albert.

"You will never hear the end of it. If you do this you need to be prepared for what may follow."

"What may follow?" echoed Albert. "That sounds ominous."

"Look, leave it to me. I'll go find somewhere to put this and we'll see. It may take some time tracking it before it reaches a destination though. That is, if this tracker does go abroad."

"Will the battery in it last long enough?" asked Clive.

"Up to 10 years," said Ben as he walked away.

Throughout their conversation, regular recycling customers were coming and going. Getting their coffees and sitting at Joe's tables. As Albert and Clive were finishing their lunch, they noticed Ms Hunter sitting herself at the empty table nearest to Joe's skip café and placing her lunchbox on it. After a few minutes, Joe brought over two coffees and sat with her.

"Shouldn't we be getting back to work?" said Albert.

"Yes. But I want to see what happens here, so we'll stay for a minute. Do you notice anything different about Ms Hunter today?"

Albert looked over at her. "No."

"Look again. Look at her face … carefully."

Albert squinted at her. "No."

"I just saw her in the office doing her lipstick and brushing her hair etc. I've never seen her do that before. And did you see her nails? She's painted them custard yellow. They match the colour of Joe's skip! They've never been anything other than orange before. Can you hear what they're saying?"

"No. Wait. Are you saying that Ms Hunter … and Joe …?"

"Yes. Think about it. It makes sense. Both single. Both about thirty."

"Should we be worried?"

"I don't know, but I don't like it. I don't like change. Come on. Let's get back to work."

* * *

"Do you mind if I join you, Ms Hunter?" asked Joe, approaching her table.

She flicked her straight, black shoulder length hair, aimed a warm smile at him and indicated the chair Joe was about to sit in anyway. "Please do."

"Look, I can't keep calling you Ms Hunter."

"It's Billie. Call me Billie. But who's going to run the café if you are sitting with me?"

"Jabby is standing in for me for a while. He offered to give up some of his lunch hour to learn a bit of the coffee trade. Says it would give him an opportunity to connect more with the customers. However, from what I have seen so far, he seems more interested in connecting with young female customers. But I owe him. He got me my mattress."

"Did he by any chance tell you why he keeps spare mattresses?"

"No, he didn't mention it."

"Good. You're better off not knowing."

"O-kay … he made these two coffees. What do you think?"

Ms Hunter was about to take a sip but stopped when she saw there was an image made with the creamy froth.

"Wow! You've made a work of art with the cream. It's an image of your skip house. It's amazing! Surely Jabby didn't do this."

"No. Jabby just made the coffee. I did the art. I did try to teach him but every time he put the cream in it ended up looking like a, shall I say, particularly male part of the body!"

She laughed. "That's Jabby, obsessed with beards."

Joe laughed.

Ms Hunter then frowned. "It's wonderful. But I can't drink this. It has milk in it and I'm vegan. I'm so sorry."

"Not a problem," said Joe. "I guessed you might be vegan so I used almond milk. Go on try it."

She took a sip this time. "Very nice indeed. You have trained Jabby well. But you guessed I was vegan? Do I look vegan?"

"That was a white lie," he grinned. "Jabby told me. And anyway, I'm vegan too and vegan lies are more environmentally friendly."

"Do you make a habit of lying? I mean, do you lie to your girlfriend?"

"I don't have a girlfriend. Not right now anyway."

Ms Hunter smiled her biggest smile yet.

* * *

Albert and Clive were up at cardboard waste shifting a stack of boxes from somebody's car. The boxes had not all been squashed so Albert was attempting to flatten them by jumping on them. This made it difficult to talk, but between each jump he managed to get out a few words.

"I was wondering …" Jump. "If people lie all the time …" Stomp. "Why do we put up with it?" Jump, stomp, trample.

"Any number of reasons. Mostly I guess, because it makes your life easier if you gloss over them. Let's see. Say the company you work for says you are next in line for promotion and when the time comes, they promote somebody else. Your job is likely to depend on you not rocking the boat. Are you going to challenge an obvious lie and risk your whole livelihood? I doubt it.

Or your partner lies to you. If you challenge them, it may spark a blazing row. Do you really want that while you eat your breakfast?

If you lie to your kids, it dodges any awkward questions without you having to talk about serious life issues with them. Many of those issues may not have an easy answer. Or the answer they need is too embarrassing to talk about.

And how about ourselves? How many of us would willingly take time out to challenge the lies we tell ourselves when, heaven forbid, we may be forced to change our minds on something? No. The vast majority will seek out the easy option. They prefer to find themselves stuck between a pillow and a soft place. And so, nothing changes."

"Are you going to challenge Ms Hunter on her intentions toward Joe then?"

"No, of course not. Where's my pillow?"

* * *

The following Monday, Ms Hunter stood in front of her desk providing an update to the staff including Joe, who by now was a kind of honorary member of staff.

"You will all be pleased to know that I checked the progress of Ben's waste tracker last Friday night and I think we can all relax in the knowledge that regulations are being followed. The tracker shows that it ended up exactly where it was supposed to be. At the waste processing plant."

"No, it's not," said Ben. "I checked just now and over the weekend the tracker headed east, to the other side of the county."

Everybody reached for their phones and opened their tracker app.

"Is this true?"

Nods around the room.

"The tracker then stopped at some remote countryside location, some kind of woodland as far as I can tell. It hasn't moved for 24 hours."

"Well, I don't know there's much we can do about that for now other than to keep monitoring. At least we have some good news. Joe's little business is doing really well. More customers coming in means we are meeting and exceeding our recycling targets for the first time ever and a small amount of money comes in to help offset expenses. All appears to be well. Although, I have to say, I tend to worry when everything seems to be going well. Any other items to discuss?"

Joe raised his hand.

"Yes Joe?"

"I could do with a few more plastic tables and chairs or benches for the café. If anyone sees something that might do, would you please save it for me? Thanks."

* * *

That lunchtime Albert and Clive once again walked straight to Joe's Café. This was seven days on the trot. Their beloved bench seemed a distant memory. Joe's was now the in-place for them. For everybody. The first table they approached had a reserved sign on it. They chose another. When Joe came over with their usual order, Clive queried it.

"People are reserving tables now Joe!?"

"It's only that one furthest away."

"Why that one?"

"Why did you want to sit there?"

Clive thought about it. "You can see what's happening around the skips from there."

"Exactly. That's why it's popular. Most of the tables only get a view of the back of the office. The customers like a table with skip views. That's another reason I need more tables. There's a spot the other side where there would be views of other skips. Rubble for example. I think that would be popular. Who doesn't like looking at rubble? If we could set up a couple of benches, like a viewing platform, we could probably charge a small amount for them to just sit and watch people dumping their stuff. There seems to be a demand for it. Oh, and we now have dog walkers coming in. One of my regulars likes to drink coffee and watch the world go by with her dog, Prince."

"Wait," said Albert, "do you know the name of this regular?"

"Yes, her name is Lucy."

"That's my aunt Lucy and her dog Prince!"

"Oh, I didn't know. Well, she's a lovely old lady. Talks a lot mind. Seems to know a lot of people in Dedbury. She's been telling her friends about us."

When Joe left them, Albert turned to Clive. "I can't believe it. Aunt Lucy's been coming here and I didn't even know! This place is becoming more popular than Tarbuck's Café in town. Next thing you know we'll be seeing regulars from the Red Lion down here."

* * *

By Friday it had become clear that Ben's tracker had not moved and did not look about to move. It was on Ms Hunter's mind and she felt she should do something. She took her lunch to Joe's café and it was not long before Joe joined her.

"So, Billie, what have you got in your lunchbox today?"

"Couscous and butternut squash salad today. You?"

"Guess."

Ms Hunter grinned. "Alright. Hmm, what do I think you might have in your lunchbox? Well, you have quite a big lunchbox." She grinned again. "I'm guessing nuts! Big ones!"

He laughed. "Better than that. Falafels!"

"What? No vegan sausage?"

He laughed again. "I think this conversation may be getting out of hand! Maybe we should change the subject."

Billie hesitated. "Actually, I …"

"What? Tell me."

She took a breath. "I was going to ask if you were doing anything at the weekend."

"Why?"

"I was wondering if you fancied going for a woodland walk. You and me. We could take a picnic."

"I'd love that. I hope it's within walking distance because I don't have a car."

"No problem. I have a car."

"This sound exciting. How far are these woods?"

"Cross county."

"I am really glad you have a car. That sounds fantastic. Bit of a drive maybe. An hour or so? You must like these woods."

"Never been there."

"Never been there? Wait. Other side of the county? Isn't that where Ben's tracker went?"

Ms Hunter donned her 'sorry' face. "Yes. I hope you don't mind, but I need to see for myself where that tracker ended up before I report any nefarious goings on to the council. And if there are indeed any dodgy doings … well, I didn't want to go alone."

Joe almost fell off his chair laughing. "That's the most romantic thing I ever heard. Basically, 'Let's go find an illegal rubbish dump together … we'll have a picnic!" He reached out and put his hand on hers. "Of course I want to come with you. Wouldn't miss it for the world. And I could do with finding some open space after living in a skip for a while."

* * *

The heartbeat of Ben's tracker brought Billie and Joe to an expansive wooded beauty spot open to the public. By the time they pulled into the car park it was almost midday. Technically, autumn had begun, but the weather was fine. Billie had decided to wear blue jeans and a custard yellow top to match her nails; the jeans in case she had to wade through any piles of trash to find Ben's tracking device. Joe also wore jeans and his usual cream tee-shirt printed with a large cup of coffee and his Café Joe logo.

A helpful sign indicated there was a picnic area beyond the trees surrounding the car park. Joe took his backpack from the car boot. Some free maps of the area were available. Billie took one.

"Hungry?"

Billie nodded. They found some chunky timber tables with bench seating and settled themselves for a bite to eat facing a small tranquil lake. More trees lined the lake, rising up the hillside beyond. The trees were mixed natives just on the turn. A patchwork of greens, coppers and yellows leeched into the water causing reflections like an impressionist painting.

"In a few weeks the leaves will turn completely and this will be glorious," said Billie, beaming.

Joe watched her face, clearly transported by the view.

"The view is pretty glorious right now," he said, cheesily. She was too lost in the moment to notice the compliment. He pulled a flask from his backpack and poured coffee into two paper cups. The coffee got her attention.

"You know, Billie, I can't help but notice the contrast between the fresh air and beauty here, which you obviously love so much, with the exact opposite where you work. What made you choose such a dirty and smelly old job?"

"I sometimes wonder, but it's not all bad. The job has some saving graces. The guys seem to need me. They are a rag-tag bunch of weirdos, but they are good hearted weirdos and that's the main thing."

"Weirdos? Misfits more like. But I know what you mean. I kind of like them. Being a misfit myself I feel like I fit in."

"You're not a misfit."

"Erm, I live in a skip."

Billie grinned. "Okay, but you're not as bad as them anyway. Look at them." She spread the fingers of her left hand and touched her thumb with the forefinger of her right.

"There's Ted. So overweight that he can hardly get up the slope to General Waste, let alone lift anything heavier than a binbag. On the other hand, he's Welsh and has the voice of an angel." She moved from thumb to forefinger, touching each of her fingers in turn as she outlined each staff member.

"Then there's Jabby. A man with a half-track mind. Can hardly keep his eyes off any woman he sees. On the other hand, women seem to have the same reaction to him. Especially when he takes his shirt off. And he dotes on that baby of his."

"And," interrupted Joe, "he has been a great help to me running the shop. And he is a great provider of mattresses."

"Hmm. Next, we have Bogsy. A big brute of a guy who can't talk to anybody without his glove puppet."

"Yeah, that is weird."

Billie continued. "But he's strong and is willing to help absolutely anybody. And where do I even start with Albert and Clive, our resident married couple?"

"They say some people get cynical in their old age. I think Clive was born cynical. I wouldn't be surprised if he had his mother's milk tested before taking it. Yet he comes up with musical commentary that's on point and entertaining.

And as for Albert, he is pretty much the opposite. Tends to believe almost anything and trusts people far too easily. Neither of them functions that well but together they seem to get by. They remind me of the two halves of a pantomime horse."

Joe laughed. "Which end of the horse is which?"

"They are interchangeable. But we can't stay here doing a psych evaluation of my staff all day, tempting though that is."

Billie opened the tracker app on her phone and studied it for a moment. Her head turned away from the lake, leftwards, eyes following the path; losing it as it turned out of sight and climbed with the tree-line up the hillside and into the distance beyond.

"We need to go this way." She rose from the table and set off.

Joe packed away his flask, dumped their paper cups and other waste in thoughtfully provided recycling bins and hurried after her.

The path wound its way around the richly planted lake edge opening up new stunning vistas at every turn. The planting created havens for waterfowl and wildlife generally. They both stopped in their tracks when a cloud of small birds flew in over the lake, wheeling around above their heads to settle in the trees and around the lake to drink. Some settled into a stand of trees in front of them. They stood speechless for several moments until Billie broke the silence.

"They say that life is a series of moments. This is one I hope to remember."

"That sounds deep. Who said that?"

"Whatever thoughts may come to you in life, one invariably finds that somebody else has had that same thought and put it into words better than you. If you can't find anyone else who said it then I claim the quote." She grinned. "The birds look like chaffinches."

"Bramblings," said Joe. "They call them the Eurasian chaffinch. Probably resting on their way north from Europe."

"You know birds?"

"A little hobby of mine. I've never seen anything like this before though. This is amazing."

They continued and eventually the path began to rise. The slope was gradual and not too demanding but after a while it became clear there was no direct route to the tracker. Billie opened the map.

"Let's think this through. If waste is being illegally dumped up here, nobody is going to be pushing it up here in a wheelbarrow. There has to be a road or track of some sort, but I don't see anything on this map."

"Try Google maps."

Billie found the location on Google maps and expanded until a track became visible. They headed toward it through the trees and eventually found it. The track was wide enough for a vehicle but the entrance was blocked by an insubstantial barrier and a sign that said 'No entry. Forestry vehicles only'.

Billie could see the path was well used and led directly to the location of the tracker. Stepping around the barrier, they continued upward. The canopy of large trees and dense foliage cast deep shade on the way forward. The temperature dropped and their mood changed. The darkness appeared to intensify the closer they got to the tracker. Eventually, the trees thinned and the land opened out ahead, though the hilltop remained obscured by a misty haze.

"Looks like some early morning mist up ahead," said Joe.

"It's not morning," said Billie. "And that's no mist." She checked her app again. "It says we are very close."

Emerging fully from the woods, crow-like birds turned slowly overhead, squawking. Topping the rise, the source of the disruption of their idyll became evident. They stopped in wonder again. This time transfixed by a scene of utter devastation. The stench of foul air caught in their throats. They peered through a miasma. Before them lay a literal wasteland. A shocking expanse of desolation.

"It looks like they've filled some old quarry with waste," said Joe. A plastic wrapper blown by the wind caught against his shoe. He picked it up. "And judging by the sell-by date on this, they are still dumping."

The same gust of wind thinned the mist to reveal the garbage heap stretching several football fields into the distance.

"There must be thousands of tons of plastic here," said Joe.

"What's that?" asked Billie, pointing to an area of bubbling black liquid."

"I don't know. And at this point I don't want to know."

"Some poor creatures have fallen into it." She instinctively moved toward them but Joe held her back.

"Bramblings," said Joe. "And the black liquid isn't bubbling. The little birds are flapping their wings trying to get out. It's too late for them. That stuff is toxic. It's in their feathers."

She turned into his arms.

Joe did not know what to say "I know, you're upset,"

"I'm more than upset. I'm angry. Somebody is going to pay for this."

She took out her phone and began taking pictures. "I think we can forget picking up the tracker. It's buried … under there … who knows how deep."

Joe stared into the deep. "I'm not a religious person, but if ever there was a hell on earth, then this is it. And no creator was involved here. We made this hell all by ourselves. You know, you were saying life was a series of moments? This is one moment I am never going to forget. No matter how hard I try."

They made their way down in silence, their heads trying to process the enormity of what they had just seen. On reaching the picnic area, they saw a middle-aged woman at a stand nearby. A hand made sign said, 'No illegal dumping. Please sign the petition'.

"This lady seems like someone we should talk to," said Joe.

"Agreed."

They approached the woman and signed the petition.

"Can you spare a moment?" said Billie, "we'd like to talk to you."

They sat at a table close to her petition stand.

"We assume you are petitioning against the illegal dumping we have just witnessed right here. Can you tell us about it?"

"I would be more than happy to," said the woman.

* * *

Albert and Clive immediately realised that this Monday staff meeting would not be a normal one. Two reasons. Ms Hunter's dungarees were black. Not her usual orange. And she skipped her usual yoga routines. Her demeanour was sombre.

"Get ready for some bad news," whispered Clive.

"Why are you always so negative? Maybe it will be all good news"

"We'll see."

Ms Hunter began speaking. "I have some bad news. Very bad news."

Clive gave Albert a self-satisfied look.

"Over the weekend, Joe and I took a trip to see for ourselves where Ben's tracker ended up. The trip confirmed our worst fears. We found an enormous illegal dump in a beauty spot. It is hard to explain just how bad it was."

"Maybe I can help you there," said Ben. "My mother has been telling me about this kind of problem for months now."

"The floor is yours," said Ms Hunter.

"During lockdown, local recycling centres like this one were shut down. After lockdown, huge volumes of trash had to be processed and local authorities, ever eager to save money, allowed authorised waste removal businesses a free rein as long as they got rid of the problem as cheaply as possible. What happens is they take the plastic waste for shredding as normal and then dump the rest of it for free any place where they think they can get away with it. No questions asked by councils because they had a lot of other issues to contend with.

There is a famous example of this from Northern Ireland. A place called Mobuoy near Derry. Over just a few years, a million tons of trash was dumped at a local beauty spot. Twenty times the weight of the Titanic. An expanse of 46 football pitches. Despite complaints, the local authority did nothing. Evidence showed dumping since 2013. It wasn't discovered until 2018. The perpetrators avoided paying millions of pounds in landfill taxes.

These illegal sites don't have adequate safeguards, so they can present a significant threat to public health and the environment. The waste site in Derry is dangerously close to a river which supplies the city with drinking water. A local vet reported a sharp rise in cows getting sick and dying in the area. Rates for some types of cancer – linked to toxic waste dumping in many parts of the world, were found to be up to 80% higher than the national average."

"Surely," said Clive, "local people raised concerns with the authorities if the problem was this massive."

"The thing is," continued Ben, "many reports were made but there's this thing called fofo."

"Fofo?"

"Fear of finding out. If some government official investigated and confirmed the problem was real, they would be forced to do something about it, with all the cost and aggravation that follows. Better to leave well alone. And of course, there is evidence that some senior officials may have colluded with the criminals for money. Alternatively, there have been cases of intimidating officials to back off with threats to them and their families. We are talking big money here. Fly tipping on this scale is so lucrative it rivals the drugs trade. We are talking billions. There is even a name for the criminals involved. They call them the Ecomafia. The problem is rife in Italy. A priest there is living under armed guard because he spoke out against the Ecomafia. Someone left a bomb outside his church."

Ms Hunter stepped forward.

"And all the time, families across the land are giving their time to painstakingly sort their waste having no clue that a lot of it ends up in some toxic and apocalyptic landfill site. A woman Joe and I met yesterday was raising a petition against the illegal dumping. She was doing it because her 9-year-old son had got into the park and fell into the waste. Since then, he has been in a coma for 6 months. I can't speak for all of you, but I work in recycling not illegal dumping – and this is not what I signed up for. I know someone in the County Council and they have told me who is in charge. I was late this morning because I've just written a letter to them. I am expecting them to take immediate action on this. But if they don't, I will need a plan B. I am open to any ideas."

The staff looked shell shocked. Nobody said anything for several seconds then Albert raised his hand.

"Yes Albert?"

He lowered his hand almost as soon as he raised it.

"Sorry. I thought I had an idea, but no."

"Okay. Anyone else? If not, we wait for a response to my email."

No further ideas forthcoming, Ms Hunter ended the meeting.

* * *

At lunchtime Albert and Clive walked over to Café Joe's. They found the area was now cordoned off. A rope across the entrance meant they had to get in a queue. All customers were now met by Ben who greeted everyone saying, 'Welcome to Café Joe's, do you have a reservation?'

"Reservation!?" exclaimed Clive. "We work here!"

"That's alright," said Ben. He opened the rope barrier so they could get through. "Just checking. Follow me."

He indicated a table near the perimeter. "Here, I'll put you next to these two lady dog walkers."

They seated themselves and Albert immediately recognised one of the ladies to be his Aunt Lucy. Her dog Prince was lying calmly under the table. Albert waved to her and she waved back. She turned to the elderly lady next to her to reveal that Albert was her sister's son. Albert stepped over and offered his hand to complete the introduction.

"This is my friend Woozie," she said. "It's a nickname," she added, anticipating Albert's next question.

Woozie also had a dog with her. It was a cute looking ball of fur. The dog had a purple collar, a perfect match with Woozie's purple hair. While he made a fuss of her dog, he furrowed his brow and mouthed 'Woozie?' at Aunt Lucy. She answered his query with the all-familiar trembling hand gesture suggesting that Woozie was fond of a drink.

"And what kind of a dog are you?" said Albert to the dog.

"Shih Tzu," replied Woozie.

"Excuse me?"

"Shih Tzu."

"That's what I thought you said. And what's his name?" said Albert, still stroking the dog.

"He's called Dogzilla," said Woozie.

"Ooh, scary name," laughed Albert.

"Yes," said Aunt Lucy. "But his previous name was scarier. He used to be called Andrew, after her husband.

"What's scary about Andrew?"

"Nothing really, but recently people started to make comments when they met Prince and Andrew together, so Woozie thought it best to change it."

Woozie nodded. "I thought the new name would improve his street cred. It certainly gets attention when I shout 'Dogzilla' in the park."

Albert sat down with Clive again.

Joe came over with coffees for the two ladies. He told them how pleased he was to see them again. Complimenting Woozie on her latest hair colour, he too made a fuss of the dogs.

"Isn't he such a lovely man," said Woozie, after he walked away.

"Yes," said Aunt Lucy, "he would be. He's Brenda's eldest. You know Brenda. Always was one for manners and discipline. It was all 'spare the rod, spoil the child' in those days."

Woozie returned a blank expression and shook her head.

"Brenda. You must know Brenda. Works on checkout at the Coop."

Woozie shook her head again.

"Her sister Bertha does the meat deliveries to local care homes." She looked from side to side and reduced her voice to a whisper before her next comment. "Provides 'special' services to the butcher and gets a large erm …"

"Discount?" suggested Woozie.

"Yes, a large discount," agreed Aunt Lucy. "The 'sausage maker' some call her. You can sympathise though because her husband's doing time for handling stolen goods. Eighteen months. It's a long time without … erm …"

"A sausage?" suggested Woozie, still looking blank on Brenda and Bertha.

"Surely you know about Bertha's husband? Sold a stolen car to Lotty who lives at number 37. Police took it off her the next day but had to tow it because some teenagers stole the wheels overnight."

Woozie shook her head once more.

"Lotty! Her youngest girl works down the hairdressers. The one who left Rosa Rotwood under the dryer too long and she had to be taken to A&E."

At this point Woozie's eyes lit up. She frowned, touched her purple hair comfortingly and nodded sagely. "Ohhh … THAT Brenda. Now I know who you mean."

* * *

Albert was staring into thin air, a vacant look on his face.

"You look bored," said Clive. "What's up? Aunt Lucy's story not involved enough for you?"

"That's because I am bored. I'm up to date with YouTube."

"What do you mean?"

"I mean what I said. I'm up to date with YouTube. I've watched everything."

Clive gave him a hard stare. "Everything? That's not possible. They say you would have to watch for 18,000 years continuously, to see every video on YouTube."

"Yes, but nothing like that long if you miss out the cat videos."

Clive was about to say something scathing but Ben walked over with their coffees. Instead, he asked how Ben was liking working at the recycle centre. Ben decided to sit with them.

"Anything is better than going home," said Ben in his usual lifeless, disinterested voice.

"High praise indeed," laughed Clive.

"Oh, I didn't mean it like that. I mean it's okay, but it's not exactly something anyone would want to spend their whole life doing."

"Even higher praise. That's what Albert and I told each other 10 years ago! The thing is Ben, after hearing your in-depth explanation about the ins and outs of toxic waste earlier, it seems to us that your knowledge makes you an ideal candidate for this kind of work."

"That's what my mother wants. It's not what I want."

"So tell me, what would you rather be doing?"

"I see myself as a writer."

"A writer?" said a surprised Albert. "What do you like to write about?"

"I'm writing a novel. It's science fiction."

For the first time there was colour in Ben's normally monotone voice. Clive asked him if he could tell them anything about the plot and Ben became fully animated for the first time.

"The story is about these aliens who have ruined their own planet with the amount of waste they have created over hundreds of years. They realise if they don't take urgent action, their planet will die. So they build enormous space ships and transport it all to another solar system. There is so much trash that over time it coalesces until eventually the mass is enough to turn it into a moon with its own gravity."

"Very interesting," said Clive. "However, it sounds like you are still inspired by the world view your mother has instilled in you."

"You may be right about my mother. But they say a writer usually writes about what they know. I know a lot about rubbish."

Clive nodded. "Your story line sounds like a great idea. What happens next?"

"The aliens don't realise they upset people on a nearby planet when the new moon moves into their planet's orbit. The planet already had one moon so the arrival of the second one creates havoc with their oceans."

"Let me guess," said Clive, "the planet the aliens are dumping around is Earth. What a brilliant plot."

Ben shook his head. "No. The aliens dumping the rubbish around another planet (I call it sky-tipping in the novel), are revealed in the end to be us humans!"

"Nice twist," said Albert. "And it makes sense. If that meeting this morning is anything to go by, we humans are the problem. We will do anything to brush our rubbish under the carpet rather than actually deal with it in an honest and serious manner."

"I agree," said Clive, "I honestly don't think Ms Hunter writing to the council will change anything. Not when there is so much money involved. I mean, it would be so easy to find corruptible officials to look the other way. I'd say she has no chance."

Ben nodded in agreement. "My mother is of the same mind. She has come across those kinds of officials before. Maybe we should be thinking of a plan B."

"I think we should give plan A chance first," said Albert. "I think people will want to do the right thing once they have been confronted."

Clive and Ben exchanged glances, looked at Albert and said nothing.

* * *

"Thank you for agreeing to see me at short notice," said the fat-faced, bald, middle-aged man who sat facing Ms Hunter across her desk. "Allow me to introduce myself. I'm Savage, Stephen Savage. I work in the Council's waste management office."

The man pulled a letter from his jacket pocket and threw it down on the desk.

"What is the meaning of this?"

Ms Hunter picked up the letter and recognised it to be the one she had sent on Monday, four days earlier.

"I should think that if you read my letter, the meaning is quite plain."

"Your letter is a mistake. And it will never see the light of day." Savage spoke aggressively.

"And why might that be?"

"All you say is clearly a fabrication. I am certain you will agree."

Ms Hunter stiffened her resolve. "I certainly do not agree. I have evidence and witnesses."

Savage smiled a sly smile. "And I have evidence that you are running an unlicenced coffee shop business from these council premises. Not only that, but there have been Health and Safety violations."

"What Health and Safety violations?"

"Personal injuries sustained by various members of the public. I too have witnesses. Indeed, it is looking highly likely that said business will have to be shut down and the owner evicted from this site."

Ms Hunter gasped. "You wouldn't."

"As I said, your letter will never see the light of day. Do we understand each other?"

Savage did not wait for an answer. He rose from the desk and headed to the door. He turned to give her one last menacing look and left without closing the door. Utterly downcast, Ms Hunter slowly walked across the office to shut the door but Albert and Clive saw her and noticed her uncharacteristic despondency. They asked if they could help. She beckoned them inside and told them about her meeting with Savage.

"So you see, I am faced with a terrible dilemma. Either I report Savage and I ... we lose Joe and his café and he loses his home and maybe I even lose my job for not reporting it properly or I say nothing, the terrible waste dumping continues, toxic emanations continue and innocent people will continue to get ill and maybe even die. What do I do?"

Clive shook his head. "I don't know. But whatever you decide, we will all stand beside you."

"Don't do anything for now," said Albert. "I may have an idea."

"What idea?" asked Clive. But Albert ignored him. He marched out of the office with a determined look on his face.

* * *

Albert was angry. He walked to a quiet corner of the car park, took out his phone and sent a short WhatsApp message to someone on his contacts list. The message read simply, 'We need to talk. But not on WhatsApp'. He scribbled a name on a scrap of paper then paced up and down for several minutes before he got the familiar ping on his phone. The reply was a single word, 'Where?'.

'Meet me here after work,' Albert texted.

After everyone else went home, Albert remained behind and waited for a visitor. He did not have to wait long before the familiar sight of a shiny black limousine pulled up in front of the entrance gate. A big bruiser of a man stepped out of it and walked up to him.

"Cecil, thank you for agreeing to meet me. I am so pleased you did not go to jail with your boss."

"So am I. I am here because I owe you a debt of thanks for your involvement in getting my boss put away."

"Really? Why?"

Cecil stared at him. "That man made me wipe the pus from the exploding zits on his face."

"Enough said. Yet you still work for him," Albert nodded at the limo.

"He still pays me ... albeit at a lower wage because of reduced zit duties."

"How is Falcon enjoying jail?"

"Annoyingly well. He pays one of the guards to clean his zits now. But I expect you did not call me to talk about zits. What can I do for you?"

Albert nodded. "You're right. We have a problem with a corrupt council official." He handed Cecil the scrap of paper with a name on it. "This person has made threats against the manager here, Ms Hunter." He explained the situation. "I need someone to erm, persuade him to change his mind. Legally of course."

Cecil stared at him again. "If you wanted something that could be done legally, you would not have called me." Cecil took the note and pocketed it. "It shall be done," he said, and headed back to the limo.

* * *

After fretting all weekend over what options she had to both save Joe and yet still report the illegal dumping, Ms Hunter had barely slept. She now stood, zombie-like, ready to begin the usual Monday morning meeting. It was decision time. She was tense. Uncomfortable. She had to report to her staff and she was not happy. However, her decision had been made and there was no way she was going to allow Joe to be kicked out of his accommodation. She stood in front of her desk ready to speak when Jabby walked up to her, phone in hand.

"Before you begin, you may be interested in this news item," he said. "It's about that guy you met last week."

She took his phone and played a video clip. A BBC local news reporter was speaking.

'We are just getting reports that Stephen Savage, Head of the council's Waste Disposal department, has unexpectedly resigned. He has refused to comment to the press about his decision but colleagues are saying that he was abducted over the weekend by an unknown assailant and thrown into an illegal waste dump at a local beauty spot. Allegedly, his office had received constant complaints about the dumping and associated health risks but they had all been dismissed by Savage as hearsay. I am guessing that being thrown into the very illegal dump that you say does not exist, is hard to explain. Councillor Savage is currently in hospital being treated for chemical burns and breathing difficulty. When asked for further details, a spokesperson for Councillor Savage said, "No comment". The police are launching a full investigation into both the abduction and the illegal dumping.'

"Does that make a difference to what you were about to say?" asked Jabby.

"It certainly does. Thanks for that Jabby." The tension in her face melted away. She turned to the staff. "At last, action is going to be taken. I think, under the circumstances there should be no need to take any action ourselves. I could not have wished for a better outcome."

After the meeting Albert approached Jabby. "Thanks for doing that for me Jabby."

"No problem, but why didn't you show that report to Ms Hunter yourself?"

"Oh, you know, Clive would never let me hear the end of it."

* * *

The following Saturday, Billie and Joe returned to the damaged beauty spot to find that the area of illegal dumping had been cordoned off. A police incident van blocked the track up to it. They hiked up the hill and settled on a mound which allowed a view of the wasteland. Joe pulled a blanket from his backpack and laid it on the grass. Sitting side by side they stared ahead in silence for a while watching two men in hazmat suits prodding the waste with metal devices. Billie broke the silence with a question.

"Why do so many people do such terrible things?"

Her question was rhetorical but Joe made an effort to answer it.

"Greed. Greed, I guess." He poured coffee into two paper cups, passing one to Billie. He then opened a small cardboard box to reveal a large cupcake. Pushing a single candle into the cake he lit it with a match and passed it to her.

"What's this?"

"Happy birthday," said Joe.

"Oh, how did you know?"

"Jabby mentioned it."

"I'll be having words with him," she grinned. "But thank you."

"Come on. Blow out the candle and make a wish."

A short puff and the flame was gone. She stared out at the waste again. "Before you ask, I wished that this mess would disappear as easily as a candle flame. That's not going to happen is it."

Joe reached into his backpack once more and handed her a parcel the size of a small envelope.

"I know this isn't the most romantic of situations. I mean, a picnic by an illegal pile of toxic waste, but it's a birthday gift."

"I don't know what to say."

"Open it."

Billie carefully peeled away the wrapping. On seeing the contents, she beamed.

"Earrings! Oh, they're lovely. They're shaped like your skip. And custard yellow! My new favourite colour."

"If you look carefully, each skip is inscribed."

She looked again. "Yes, each skip has the word Joe's etched onto it in silver." She put them on. "I'm guessing these are not the kind of thing you are likely to find on Amazon."

"No. I had them specially made by a silversmith friend. I hope you like them."

Billie did not answer. She leaned over, and kissed him.

Garbo

At six foot two, the square-jawed, broad-shouldered captain of the Starship 'Contaminante' looked the epitome of a space hero. Standing on the bridge, watching the fast-approaching solar system on the large viewscreen, he felt like one too. The only fly in his ointment was his young new co-pilot who never stopped asking questions.

"I'm beginning to think they don't teach you new recruits anything these days," he said.

"Why would they? Everything on this ship is automatic. I don't know why they even need us."

"In case some unforeseen event occurs."

"What kind of unforeseen event?"

The captain sighed. "The clue is in the word unforeseen. If they could foresee it then it wouldn't be unforeseen, would it?"

The co-pilot shrugged off the slur. "So if we do get an unforeseen event, what do we do?"

"You use the controls on your console."

"What controls? There's just a single knob and a switch."

"Yes. You use the knob."

"How?"

"You fiddle with it." The captain looked embarrassed. "I don't know. They did tell me how to use it on my first trip but that was two years ago. I've never needed to use it. I thought you, with your recent training, would know how to do it."

The co-pilot could not think of a calm response to this. He was about to say, 'What training?' But he found himself asking a related question and instantly regretting it.

"What about the switch?"

"Oh, I know what that does."

The co-pilot stared silently, but quizzically, at the captain until he explained.

"It turns the windscreen wipers on."

The co-pilot now stared at the captain in disbelief.

"Remind me again why we are even having to do this. I mean, ship Earth's trash to another solar system. Seems extreme."

The captain sighed again, his square shoulders now visibly slumping.

"Evidently, they don't teach you anything. Let me enlighten you. For a thousand years or so we dumped our trash in space in our own solar system and all seemed well until large chunks of it eventually found its way back to Earth. The trash was so toxic that it polluted the Earth's already polluted atmosphere as it burned up. So, once the hyperdrive was invented a few years ago, it seemed logical to ship it all to another solar system and release it into that system's gravity well so there would be no chance of the trash finding its way back to Earth. And we have been doing that ever since, 50 million tons of waste at a time."

"Oh, yeah," said the co-pilot. "Makes sense. But what if there is some kind of intelligent life in that system?"

"They thought of that. That's why they chose to dump it all near a planet devoid of intelligent life. In that way we don't pollute any of the other planets, just in case."

"Is that the planet they call Garbo?"

"Yes Garbo, because of all the garbage there. And I've had enough questions for now. I'm going to get something to eat. Call me when we get there." He turned to walk away.

"Just one more question. Something that's been frazzling my brain," said the co-pilot.

The captain turned back and glowered at him. "Yes?"

The co-pilot pointed at two long, thin metal arms attached to the exterior of the ship's view screen.

"Why does a space ship need windscreen wipers?"

"Space dust," said the captain, marching off.

* * *

"Effluenza, check this out," said Gunk, adjusting his monitor with three of his six legs.

"What is it?" snapped Effluenza.

"They're at it again."

"What?" Effluenza was in the middle of arranging lunch for them both and, due to the school holidays, also for their 175 children and did not want to be distracted.

"It's them," said Gunk, "the aliens. They're back. And they are dumping their trash in our space again."

"So?"

"So, I see an opportunity."

"I thought you didn't want to get involved." Effluenza finished filling a large, flat-bottomed, circular container. Around its circumference poked out short, narrow tubes numbering exactly 175. No more, no less. Having prepared the kids' drinks, she looked up at him, frowned and buzzed her wings at him to show her displeasure.

"Our esteemed leader, first minister Crud, has given specific instructions. Nobody is to interfere with the aliens." She turned away from him to shout in the direction of the kid's nest on the upper level.

"Come get your juice kids."

This prompted an instant response from Cess and Gloop, their two eldest.

"What flavour, mother?"

"It's your favourite, Mulled Slurry."

A loud buzz followed her announcement as 175 pairs of wings sprang into action and the kids swarmed down to take their places around the circular bowl of slurry. As each of them took their places around the perimeter, the buzzing died away only to be replaced by loud slurping as 175 long tongues unfurled along 175 tubes.

Effluenza smiled briefly at her offspring but the smile faded when she turned back to speak to Gunk again.

"Now, I have 175 food helpings to dish out. Are you going to help me or are you just going to stand around thinking up crazy schemes as usual?"

Gunk, oblivious to what she was saying, continued with his earlier conversation.

"First minister Crud doesn't know what he's talking about. And anyway, you haven't heard my idea. I'm talking about making money out of these aliens. So much money we could hire some home help. The help would look after the kids and you could relax. Take the weight off your legs."

For the first time Effluenza looked interested. "I know I am going to regret this, but let's hear it."

Gunk grinned, stroked his two antennae with his front legs and flew over to her.

"Okay, so we know these aliens are dumping their waste here and in normal circumstances that would be seen as a bad thing. However, what the aliens don't know, is that the kind of waste they bring us comprises the perfect kind of toxicity for us to feed off. That's why Crud wants to leave well alone."

He paused to make sure Effluenza was still following him.

"Go on," she said.

"Well, of course we all want this free food they keep bringing us, but the Aliens don't know we want it. They are just dumping it."

He now moved to stand directly in front of her and stared into her beautiful, dark, space-black, compound eyes.

"I propose we go to meet them and tell them we are prepared to accept their trash, but only for a price. What do you think?"

"I think you're crazy. How would they pay us? What else have they got that we might want? And nobody has even seen these aliens, only their ships. What if they look disgusting?"

Gunk smiled. "That wasn't a no then! Look, how can anyone know what these aliens have got until we ask them? And as to their looks, we've all watched sci-fi movies. Aliens always look just like us, but with weird looking heads."

Effluenza did not look convinced. He tried once more. "We could go see them right after lunch. We'll take the kids with us. You're always saying we don't take them into space often enough. It will be educational."

"Oh, all right then, as long as you think it will be educational."

Gunk grinned again, reached out with his front legs and stroked her antennae. "And when we get back tonight, maybe we could have some bumpy-jumpy."

"The trip, yes. But bumpy-jumpy? In your dreams. We already have 175 children and they're waiting for their lunch."

* * *

The captain of the starship 'Contaminante' was most surprised to get a call from his co-pilot so early. He glanced at his cabin computer which buzzed with the message and at the same time indicated they were nowhere near the drop-off point. He had to read the message twice to be sure he'd read it correctly.

Urgent. Come to the bridge. Some aliens wish to talk to us.

He was at the bridge within minutes.

"What's going on? Report."

"We've received an unexpected communication on a non-standard frequency."

"What does the message say?"

"I have no idea."

The captain gave his co-pilot a withering look.

"Then how do you know it's from aliens?"

"Well, where else would it be from?

"So why is it from aliens and not just from some random source?"

"Listen, the message is still coming through."

There followed a strange string of buzzing noises which sounded more like electrical interference than an actual message.

The captain looked excited for once. "I agree, there appear to be patterns to this signal. Maybe this is the unforeseen event we were waiting for, you know, the reason we are here on the ship. Do you know where the message is coming from?"

The co-pilot twiddled with his knob. He had barely touched it when a global map of the planet Garbo leapt onto the view screen. A red pulsating light glowed at a location in space above the planet's southern land mass.

"There," pointed the co-pilot, unhelpfully.

"Maybe we should send an acknowledgement."

"And how would I do that?"

The captain thought about it. "Oh, I remember now. That knob of yours isn't really a knob. It's a microphone. You just tell the computer what you want to do."

The co-pilot gave him a hard stare.

"Alright, now we're getting somewhere. What shall I tell it to do?"

"Try saying acknowledge message and translate," said the captain.

The instant these words left the captain's mouth the message became intelligible.

"Honoured aliens, welcome to our planet. I am First Minister Gunk and would like to welcome you personally. My ship is on its way to you with a welcoming party."

"Cancel transmission," said the co-pilot. "What do we do now?"

"I suppose we better meet them."

"Really? We have been dumping trillions of tons of toxic waste around these alien's planet for years and you think we should just wait here for them to catch us?"

"Well, if we run, they might zap our ship with some kind of alien ray gun. Anyway, they sound friendly. 'Honoured aliens, welcome to our planet', they said."

"Open transmission," said the captain. "Greetings! We come from a planet called Earth. Earth people are called humans. I am the captain of this space ship, the 'Contaminante'. We will be pleased to meet you. Shall we come to you?"

"No. We are already close to your ship. Please wait there. We are hoping that you can trade goods with us and in exchange, we will allow you to continue dumping your toxic waste here."

"Cancel transmission," said the co-pilot again. "Now what do we do? They want payment for our trash dumping."

"Don't panic. There must be something Earth has that they need."

"Yeah? Like what? I can't see what Earth has an excess of … other than dodgy drugs or carbon dioxide. We have a great deal of carbon dioxide."

"How should I know? They could be desperate for pencil sharpeners or Tippex as far as we know. Nobody uses them anymore. We just wait here like they said and we'll find out. By the way, do we know what these aliens look like?"

"No. The feed was sound only, but I wouldn't worry about it. We've all watched sci-fi shows. Aliens always look just like us, but with weird looking heads."

* * *

"Wow!" said Gunk, as his ship approached the alien trash transporter. "Their ship is massive. And that's just their ship, not to mention the masses of trash they are hauling. How close are we Effluenza?"

"Very close. We can see their view screen. How can they not see our ship?"

"Okay, send them a message. Tell them we are here."

"Done."

"What do they say?"

Effluenza waited for the alien's response.

"They say they don't see us."

"How is that possible? We are hovering right in front of them. They can't see what's in front of their own mandibles. Message them again."

"Done. Same response. They still don't see us."

Gunk was frustrated. Okay, we will go right up to them."

"We can't go any nearer, we might compromise our ship."

"I mean, we will go to them. I'll take the kids with me. Kids, make sure your space suits are fastened up tight and follow me."

Gunk donned the helmet of his own space suit, then he and his 175 space-suited offspring left their ship through the airlock and launched themselves toward the alien ship, leaving only Effluenza behind.

* * *

The captain carefully considered the rapidly evolving situation. He addressed his co-pilot.

"The thing to remember here is that there is a strict protocol issued to all starship captains, to be applied in the event of first contact with aliens. At all costs, we must treat them with the utmost respect. Whatever you do, don't upset them. Have you got that?"

"Utmost respect. Don't upset them. Got it."

The captain squinted at the view screen. "How can we not see them? They are supposed to be very close."

"I don't know, but the view screen seems to be dirty. It's getting covered by hundreds of small, pebble-sized bits of space debris. It is obscuring the view."

Together, the captain and his co-pilot had the same idea. "The windscreen wipers!" They exclaimed. The switch was pressed, the wipers swept across the viewscreen and 176 pebble-sized bits of space debris were flung violently into space.

"Now, let's have a look for these aliens again."

* * *

"And that's all I've written so far," said Ben, after he finished reading his story to Albert and Clive.

"That's it? But what happened to Gunk and his family?" asked a concerned Albert. "Somebody has to save them."

Ben gave Albert the kind of hard stare normally dished out only by Clive.

"Isn't that like asking what happened to the Cheshire Cat in Alice in Wonderland?"

Albert ignored the comment and continued to look at Ben as if the missing Gunk and his family were his own.

"Alright then, let me think. Hmm, well of course, Gunk's partner Effluenza is still in the mothership. She sees her family being thrown into space in all directions then spends a couple of hours chasing them all down to bring them safely back to the mothership. After that, they go to stay with her Uncle Fester who has an observatory on Moonbase Blister."

Albert let out a relieved sigh and smiled.

Message from a Bottle

"Where's Ms Hunter?" said Albert.

"Yes, where is she?" asked Clive. "I want to see if she's wearing those skip earrings again. The ones Joe gave her. She's worn them every day since she got them. I think there's something going on with those two."

"More importantly, where's Joe? I need my coffee," said Jabby.

The staff were gathered in the office, waiting for the Monday morning meeting to begin.

"Has anybody checked Café Joe's?" asked Clive.

Jabby volunteered. "I'll go." He left the office and returned a couple of minutes later with a puzzled look on his face.

"Joe's not there … and his bed hasn't been slept in!"

Just then, Ms Hunter walked in.

"We're worried about Joe," said Jabby. "He didn't sleep in his bed last night and we can't find him anywhere."

Ms Hunter smiled at him reassuringly. "Calm down Jabby. Joe will not be in this morning because he has a job interview."

"Job interview? What's wrong with his job here?"

"He said right from the start it was only going to be temporary. That skip of his is hardly ideal to run a business from, let alone live in."

Jabby was shaking his head. "But he didn't sleep in his bed!"

Ms Hunter sighed. "If you must know, he slept at my place last night. Alright?"

This prompted a chorus of 'Ooohs' from the staff.

"Calm down lads. It was just so he could shower early at mine and arrive fresh for his interview."

"Did he need a *cold* shower?" laughed Jabby.

She shook her head. "I am not going to dignify that with a response. Listen up everyone, head office has sent us a video to watch. It's all about AI. Unfortunately, the video is longer than our allotted meeting time. They say it is super important, so have asked us all to watch it at the end of the day. Hands up anyone who is happy to stay late."

Not a single arm was raised.

"They are paying overtime."

Every hand shot into the air.

"Jabby, as Joe's trusted number two, why don't you get coffees for us all. We now have half an hour of free time to kill." She glanced over at Ted, sitting in the corner looking glum.

"Listen everybody, I think we all need to give our support to our colleague Ted who, as some of you may know, is struggling through a time of extreme adversity."

"What's the matter Ted?" asked a shocked Albert.

"I don't want to talk about it," said Ted.

Ms Hunter walked over to Ted and put her arm around his shoulders. "It's alright Ted, we are here for you." She turned to the staff and whispered. "His doctor has told him he needs to go on a diet."

"Oh, I thought it was something serious," said Albert.

Ted gave him a withering look.

"What I meant to say was … that's awful," said Albert.

"I know," replied Ted, "It's the cake. I suppose I am my own worst enemy. Cake has always been my Achilles stomach."

When Jabby returned with the coffees, Ms hunter announced that in an effort to cheer Ted up and help him through his diet days, she had asked Clive to write a song for him and she hoped Ted would sing it for them now.

Clive handed a sheet of paper with some words on it to Ted.

"If you don't recognise the tune, think the movie 'The Thomas Crown Affair', but instead of windmills, it's diets."

Ted glanced at the first verse and smiled. "Yes, I know it. Thanks Clive."

"My pleasure." The staff sipped their coffees while Ted sang.

The diets of my mind

Down
Goes my mayo covered sandwich
And the mountain on my plate
Why did thinness go so quickly
Was it something that I ate
When I look into the mirror
I am shocked that I've become
No longer wholly human
I'm half man and half cream bun

Why can't the food I love
Be just as wonderful to taste
Yet not contain the fat
That adds the inches to my waist
Like the sausages I find
In the diets of my mind

There's a tunnel food must follow
It's a tunnel going south
Needing food to fill the hollow
Past my ever-open mouth
Like the chocolate covered doughnut
That's been dipped in double cream

I wake up in the night
To find it wasn't all a dream

I remember in my youth
I was a fit and thinner man
Now my inner bread is buttered
Overspread with inner jam
Just like the sausages I find
In the diets of my mind

All the gravy on the pastry
All the ketchup on the chips
Call to arms a million calories
To march upon the hips
Diners eating in a bistro
Diners in a restaurant
Are all taking second helpings
They can order what they want
And as I look on in envy
Through my salad I can't bear
To eat another cracker
Is like biting on thin air
From the jug of my resistance
The will to diet, though I try
Is spilling out like custard
On some home-baked apple pie

There are tables set before me
Filled with half forbidden food
Tempting never fattening
Swallowed hardly even chewed

I eat food of every kind
Like the sausages I find

All in the diets of my mind

* * *

By lunchtime Joe had returned from his job interview and normal café service had resumed. He brought coffees over to Albert and Clive at what was now their regular table. The one with the skip view.

"How did the interview go?" asked Albert.

"Great. I got the job! Its manager of an existing café in town called Tarbucks. They are setting up a second café in a new location and want someone to manage the existing one."

The change averse Albert, looked unhappy about it.

"We are so pleased for you," said Clive, glossing over the moment as best he could.

"Pity about Ted being on a diet," said Joe. "Especially now I'm trialling a new recycle centre themed food line."

"Really?"

"Yes. My dream is to run my own café one day, a proper one and because business has gone so well here, I decided that my new place will have the same environmental theme, but it would have to include food. So, I am putting together a menu and one section will be titled Junk Food. The great thing is that the owner of Tarbucks is happy to let me try it there if it works here.

I already have one or two menu options. I will include things like bin-baguettes, trashed potatoes and dumplings. Like to try a bin-baguette?"

Albert and Clive looked at each other, then back to Joe.

"Sounds delicious," said Albert, unconvincingly. "Do they come with cheese?"

"Yes."

"Make that two then," said Clive.

"Good. I'll bring them over and you can let me know what you think."

Albert waited until Joe was out of earshot before speaking to Clive.

"I don't want him to leave. Where am I going to get my coffee from?"

"You could always make your own."

"That's crazy talk."

Clive gave Albert a medium-hard stare.

"So, what do you think about all this AI palaver?" said Albert, changing the subject. "I heard it was going to be a good thing. Advancing civilisation. All our problems will be solved."

"That's not what I heard. I heard AI will take all our jobs then could possibly wipe out the whole of humanity. But apart from that, it will probably be okay."

Albert gasped. "Surely they won't let that happen. I thought the emphasis was on *Intelligence*."

"Intelligent it may be, but it's not foolproof. And the world has plenty of fools. Take the recent 'Dollhouse' incident."

"I don't know of it."

Clive slurped his coffee before telling Albert the story. Albert winced.

"I bet AI doesn't slurp its coffee," he said.

"Let me see. The Dollhouse incident. Well, it started when this American kid, a six-year-old girl called Brooke, ordered a dollhouse and a pile of cookies through an Amazon Alexa. All she did was ask for the products. Amazon charged the purchase to Brooke's parents and they were delivered a day or so later."

"That's terrible," said Albert. "What did her parents do when they got the bill?"

"It was pretty easy for them to work out what had happened so they added extra parental controls."

"Problem solved then. The parents were just idiots. AI is innocent."

"Maybe," said Clive, "but as I was saying, there are an awful lot of idiots in this world."

"What do you mean?"

"That wasn't the end of it. The local tv news channel picked up the story and broadcast it on one of their daily shows. At one point the news anchor said, "I love the little girl saying, 'Alexa order me a dollhouse.'" So guess what. This triggered Alexa devices in the homes of various viewers, to order dollhouses. I bet the dollhouse maker was well pleased. I rest my case."

Albert frowned. "But surely AI must be good for something. Maybe it could help Ted with his diet."

"I doubt it. I was chatting with Ted the other day and I know for a fact that he intends to go back to his normal eating pattern as soon as he finishes his decorating."

"Decorating?" said Albert. "At least he will be getting some exercise. Is he decorating the whole house?"

"No. Just his cake room."

"Ted has a cake room?!"

"Yes, he said this will be the only time the room will be clear of cakes so it is the ideal time to decorate."

Joe delivered their cheese bin-baguettes. They ate, sipped their coffees and stared at the long line of cars advancing around the skips like a slow-moving juggernaut of junk.

"It won't be the same when Joe leaves," said Albert.

"No. What will we do?"

"I think I would like to go visit our old bench tomorrow. Just for old times' sake."

Clive nodded. "Yes, let's do that. Maybe the bench misses us."

They bit into their bin-baguettes in synchrony. They chewed in synchrony. They stared ahead in synchrony. The line of cars edged forward. And the skips slowly filled.

* * *

After closing time, the staff reconvened in the office to watch the video about the implications of AI on recycling. Any reluctance they may have had, completely countered by the thought of overtime payment.

When it was over, Ms Hunter asked if anyone had any questions.

Many hands went up, including Bogsy's be-puppeted one.

"I'll take all your questions in turn. Yes Bogsy?"

"Will the overtime be at normal rate, time and a half or at weekend rate?" he squeaked.

Ms Hunter sighed. "Normal rate Bogsy. Who wants to ask their question next?"

She looked around the room and nobody raised their hand. She sighed again.

"You were all going to ask the same question?!"

Shifty looks.

"Does anybody have an AI related questions or comments?"

Blank looks.

"Nobody? The main gist of the film was to reassure us all that AI would not be taking over our jobs. Surely that was good news."

"I'd say the opposite," said Clive. "One of my rules is never believe anything Head Office tells you, unless its officially denied. They are saying no redundancies, so that means there is no hope for our job security in the long term."

"Thanks for that Clive. I am sure everyone is much happier to know that. Surely someone has something positive to say."

Albert raised his hand.

"Yes Albert."

"That film suggested that one day AI might be clever enough to run the government. But if AI can do *anything*, what if it becomes capable of deception?"

"Then it could *definitely* run the government," said Clive.

"Is there nobody with anything sensible to say?" asked a frustrated Ms Hunter.

Ben put his hand up. "I would like to say something. I have a confession to make."

Everyone looked at Ben.

"Does it have anything to do with AI?" asked Ms Hunter.

Ben nodded. "Yes. You all remember the tracking device I put in our waste? The one that eventually found its way to that illegal dump? Well, before I did that, my mother slipped another tracker in with the plastic. It was that day she came here to investigate using this place for her Greener Party meetings."

"I gave her a guided tour before our meeting," said Albert. "I remember her throwing some rubbish into one of our skips. That was sneaky."

"Sneaky. Yes. That's one word for my mother. Not the word I would use. Anyway, I can now reveal what happened to it."

He paused.

"Go on then," said Albert. "Where is it?"

"Well, it will be easier if I show you." He pulled a Flash Drive from his pocket and plugged it into the office laptop.

"The second tracker was not like the first. It was a state-of-the-art device controlled by AI. It was flattish and fixed to the inside of a clear plastic drink container with its camera looking out of the side of the bottle. The AI includes a progress chart so you can follow its journey across Europe. I've speeded it up."

Ben pressed play and the staff gathered around the laptop to watch. A map of the UK appeared, centred on Dedbury, then after a few seconds a thin red line wandered around main roads across the UK until it stopped at one of the authorised processing centres.

Ben explained that the device's camera would be triggered to record any close encounters and as if on cue, the map disappeared in favour of a short recording. The scene was a vast yard at a processing plant where it seemed evident that the device was pointed at the side of an enormous cubed bale of plastic at ground level. A tattered and crushed mess of filthy mixed plastic faced the onlookers.

"That's disgusting," said Albert, "I can't think of anything worse."

However, before the onlookers could make out any more details, the bale was blocked when a fork lift truck collided with it. The bale wobbled then stabilised. The driver was heard to say, "Who put that bale there? Where's my beer? Oh, there it is."

Then the driver could clearly be seen bending over in his truck to look for his beer. Too clearly. A pink moon of flesh filled the screen as his trouser belt struggled with the angle and slipped.

"Ew," came the united response from the audience.

"Just when you thought you couldn't imagine anything worse," said Clive, grinning.

"Maybe I should fast forward this bit," said an embarrassed Ben.

"Yes you should," said Ms Hunter.

"The faster the better, "said Albert.

The UK map filled the screen again and the red line continued its journey until it got to a port on the east coast.

"It stays here for a couple of days," said Ben, "then it crosses the channel to the Netherlands and stays there for another couple of days."

He fast forwarded again. The red line began to move across Europe. Ben continued his commentary.

"The tracker is travelling along a German autobahn here and it stops again at a waste processing site at a place called Zielona Gora just inside Poland. This makes commercial sense if you bear in mind that landfill in the UK costs around £100 a ton but in Poland only £20 to £30 a ton. It should be noted that the UK government give as much support to exporting trash as to processing it locally.

However, this is not the end of the journey. This seems to be a huge warehouse complex where waste waits to be sent on. I lost the signal here for a few days but it suddenly began transmitting again from a place in South East Turkey near a city called Adana close to the coast. I researched this and it seems that a huge amount of waste from all over Europe ends up there. Not just from the UK. Turkey has become known as Europe's rubbish dump.

In theory the waste then gets properly processed but Turkey does not yet have the infrastructure to deal with it all. Currently only about 20% of plastic gets recycled in Turkey. The rest gets burnt or dumped.

From here the tracker gets moved to a small village close to the Seyhan river. Some 30 years ago, the government decided to establish a landfill site there. Locals were forced to give up animal husbandry in their village due to the adverse effects of the dump and began collecting waste there instead."

At this point the tracker must have had a close encounter again because it set off another recording. A giant eyeball filled the screen, followed by a giant beak and a disturbing view down a seagull's gullet. The staff recoiled again as they watched the scene of the dump below as the gull took flight with the tracker. Literally a bird's eye view.

From above, the extent of a devastated landscape became evident. Clouds of dust and heavy smoke hung in the air with seagulls moving through it all, circling above acres of plastic and other unidentifiable waste. Through the smoke, barely visible, some villagers rummaged through the detritus.

"They say these villagers get paid less than £10 a day collecting plastic. They also separate metal and paper. They can sell this to recycling companies. But by the time these villagers get to the waste, it has already been sorted once by people elsewhere who have already taken the best of it."

The aerial view suddenly juddered as the seagull attempted to swallow the plastic covered tracker. When it gave up, the device fell awkwardly into the river.

"I assume that's the end of it," said Ms Hunter. "At least I hope so. All this is awful."

"Sadly no," said Ben. "The signal dies for a while again but then comes back to life as it finds its way down the river into the Med. Then this happens."

The next time the tracker's recording device switched itself on it was in the sea, caught up with a mess of nylon netting wrapped around the front flipper of a loggerhead turtle. The image was poor but it was very clear that the turtle was struggling to pull itself through the water.

"I don't think I can bear this," said Ms Hunter.

"Me neither," said Albert.

"Nor I," echoed Ben. "It was swimming like this for mile after mile. In the end I called somebody at a charity called Nature Trust in Malta. They rescue animals, including turtles. I gave them the GPS location and they sent a fishing boat out. The next encounter on the recording is when the fishing boat turns up. Watch."

The next image appeared through a great splash as the turtle was pulled out of the sea with its tangled netting hanging around its flipper. Then a closeup of the nostril of a grizzled, frowning fisherman as he leaned in to study the problem. He scratched his ragged beard then reached for a knife. The nylon net had dug into the turtle's flesh so deeply it had caused a gash. The fisherman wielded the knife with great care and skill until the obstruction could be removed. He studied the deep cut in its flipper and carefully placed the turtle in a large container with sea water in it. The final view was from the bottom of a bin looking up at the now smiling fisherman.

"And that's it," said Ben, removing the Flash Drive. "It's actually illegal to export plastic waste unless it's going to be recycled, but Greenpeace investigators have found British plastic dumped by the side of the road, abandoned in illegal dumps or even set on fire in both Turkey and Malaysia. Mandatory digital waste tracking won't be introduced by the government until April 2025. The trouble is that simply tracking it isn't enough. It's what happens to the waste when it gets there. Especially if it ends up in some far-flung country with low standards."

"Do we know what happened to the turtle in the end?" asked Ted.

Ben nodded. "It was taken back to the Nature Trust in Malta. They treated its wounds, allowed it to recover then released it back into the sea. However, I suspect that the millions of conscientious recyclers in this country do not expect they are spending all their time separating their plastic only for it to end up cutting through the limbs of some poor creatures half way round the world."

"This has all been so depressing," said Ms Hunter. "Sometimes I wonder why we bother doing what we do. Is everything we do here really all pointless?"

"Not everything," said Albert.

"What then? Name one thing we do here that isn't pointless."

Albert racked his brain. "Health and Safety," he said.

Ms Hunter groaned.

"Is that all? Is that all we have achieved these last few years? Learned how to do risk assessments and keep a record of injuries! But it's more than that. What has happened to this country? Britain used to be known as 'a green and pleasant land'. It was the country of Alfred the Great, of Shakespeare, of … the Wombles. Look at us now, a country illegally dumping half our garbage in our own back yard and exporting the other half to ruin the rest of the world too."

"Wombles?" queried Ben.

"Probably before your time," said Albert to young Ben. "They were an early group of furry recyclers famous for cleaning up Wimbledon Common."

"Furry?" said Ben.

"It's a long story," said Albert.

"I'm no Shakespeare," said Clive, "but when I look around at what we have achieved here, I am not at all downhearted. In spite of what you all may think, I see this Recycle Centre of ours as a small island of hope in a sea of cynicism and indifference. We should be proud of ourselves. If Shakespeare were alive today, he might have a few words to say about it."

Clive got up and stood next to Ms Hunter at the front. She sat in his empty chair as he said his piece.

This toxic tide of things, this septic isle
This mound of muck, this site of scrap
This yearned for Eden, this garden of grime
This den of dust built surely by our sweat
With Health and Safety foremost in our mind
This happy smiling crew, we favoured few

This jewel of junk set in a ring of rubble
Marries our aspirations to our clean air
And divorces our dreams from our despair
Against this endless tempest of trash
This blessed spot, this dump, this tip, this wasteland

* * *

The following day, Albert and Clive fulfilled their own promise to themselves and headed to their old bench across the road from the recycle centre with their lunch. When they got to the front gate, Albert was shocked at what he saw.

"Look!" He pointed at their bench. "There are people snogging on our bench. Our bench!"

"Those aren't people," said Clive. "That's Joe and Ms Hunter."

"Really? We better go back," said Albert.

"We better go forward," said Clive.

They crossed the road as noisily as possible causing the cuddlesome couple to look up, slightly embarrassed, but mostly pleased with themselves.

They got up giggling and started to head back to work but not before Ms Hunter turned to them and put her finger to her lips in the all-familiar 'shush' gesture.

Albert and Clive settled on the bench and stared at them in silence as the couple headed back, holding hands all the way until they were through the gates. They continued staring ahead even when they were long out of sight.

"What are you thinking?" said Clive.

Albert chewed on his cheese bin-baguette, scratched the stubble on his chin and furrowed his brow.

"I'm thinking these bin-baguettes taste better than they sound. And I was thinking maybe I should try some of that

'Litta Bread and Dip' from his new menu. What are you thinking?"

"I'm thinking Joe is going to move in with Ms Hunter and he'll get this new job and everything will change."

"I don't like change," said Albert. "Things never seem to change for the better. It's always for the worse."

"That's right," said Clive. "We should always take comfort in the knowledge that no matter how bad things may seem, things could always be worse."

Bonus Stories

Infestation

Balthazar Binko blinked twice when the message came up on his vid-screen. The convenience of an entertainment and messaging system which can materialise in front of your eyes wherever you happen to be, is something to be admired. However, when a message pops up in the midst of attending to bodily functions, it can be disconcerting. Especially when the message is a command to meet with Earth's highest authority, the Secretary General of the United Planets. To actually meet her. In person. Balthazar was so shocked he might have wet himself had he not already been attending to that very matter.

It was moments like this when he thought the ancient communication device known as a 'mobile phone' might be preferable. Not that he would ever say this to anyone. In the year 3024 his obsession with the past generally made him the focus of mockery. What to do? What to do? Clearly rattled, he decided on the best course of action and addressed the vid-screen.

"Call Wanda."

Within seconds his vid-screen filled with the face of his long-time partner, but something seemed amiss. Her face pulsated with colour like a Space Age disco.

"Balti, what do you think of my new makeup?"

He frowned. "I don't seem to be able to focus on your face properly."

"That's because I'm wearing the latest colour changing lipstick and eye shadow! I have them in 'Disco Mode'. Plus, I am trying that new product everyone's been talking about, Digi-face. I can change my whole face whenever I like. She waved a hand across her face and now looked vaguely Egyptian. This is my Cleopatra face, what do you think?"

"I think you've been a victim of pyramid selling." Balthazar pulled a face of his own. "It's disconcerting. Put your old face back. I need your advice urgently."

Wanda drew her hand across her face again and the effects stopped.

"How's that?" she said. "Wait. Are you calling from the bathroom?"

"Never mind that. I've just been called by the office of the Secretary General of the United Planets. I've been summoned to a meeting! A real meeting, not a vid-call."

"Really? When?"

"Just now."

"No, I mean when do you have to go?"

"This afternoon!"

Wanda's face displayed shock. Real shock, not digital shock.

"What have you done?"

"Nothing. Why would they want to see me? I'm just a minor functionary in a government department everyone despises and most people don't even know exists."

"Not everyone despises your department. Only most people."

"Who? Tell me one person who doesn't despise the Department of Waste Management."

Wanda smiled sweetly. "Me." She blew him a kiss and a digital X appeared on screen heading toward him but fading away at the last minute.

"You must have done something wrong," she said. "Think."

"I have thought and there's nothing. Nothing ever happens …"

Balti stopped midsentence. "Except … Wait. There was one piece of news this week. Apparently some thicko Starship captain managed to mess up a first contact with aliens. The first 'First Contact' ever! I had to make a report on it."

"What happened?"

"The captain doesn't know. His ship got a communication. Messages were exchanged. A meeting agreed on. But the aliens never showed up. A complete mystery he says."

"It has to be that," said Wanda.

"But why? It was a meeting that never took place."

"Want me to come with you?"

"You can't. They want to see me and me alone," he gulped.

"My advice to you, is don't play the victim. They wouldn't summon you if they didn't need you. How are you going to get there?"

"They are sending a transport."

"Then all I can do is wish you luck."

Balthazar cut contact, deciding to review the ship's recording of the first contact once more. It seemed as mysterious as ever until he noticed something. He addressed the vid-screen.

"Reverse video at half speed. Stop. Magnify ship's screen and enhance. Stop."

He began to see detail not seen previously.

"Magnify again and enhance. Stop."

He stared at the vid-screen in disbelief.

* * *

Analiza Yildipeg gazed out of the massive window of her massive office. Massive to emphasise the importance of her position as Secretary General of the United Planets. Staring out across the city from the 200th floor of Government Tower, the tallest building in Star City, there was much to see. On a clear day like today, shiny, tall towers receded into the distance in every direction. A testament to the prosperity accruing from her leadership. The only blot on the horizon being a hazy mist rising above the outskirts of the city. This was from the city dump. The waste had built up over the last week and regular citizens were not happy about it.

She diverted her gaze downward. Far, far below at ground level, she imagined there might be some of those regular citizens walking about. If there were, they may as well be imaginary since from this height they could not be seen. In the grand scheme of things, they were like ants. Smaller than ants, and right now, as much of a nuisance, complaining about odours and vermin infesting the city dump. In the airspace between, aerial transports shuttled here and there between the tall buildings. One of those transports approached Government Tower, hovered for a moment for a security check, then touched down on landing pad 200. Her assistant would meet the occupant and bring him to her.

There were times when Analiza felt every one of her 134 years, and this was one of those times. She hated having to talk to junior functionaries and her assistant was ushering one of them into her office. Even worse, it was a baby, a nondescript young drone in his forties. Nevertheless, she pasted on her professional smile.

"Welcome. I am Analiza Yildipeg, Secretary General of the United Planets."

"Balthazar Binko, manager of the Department of Waste Management."

"Thank you for coming."

"Did I have a choice?"

"I will ignore that. Balthazar? That is an unusual name. What were your parents thinking?"

"I am not responsible for my unusual name, Analiza Yildipeg." He emphasised the first half of her first name. "And I have no parents, I'm a Tuber.

"Oh. You're one of those. Conceived out of a test tube. How quaint."

He remembered Wanda's advice. Don't be a victim.

"I might remind you that these days we Tubers outnumber you two to one. Have you brought me here to exchange insults or do you want something?"

"What are you doing about the city dump? There have been complaints. Bad odours and an infestation of rats."

"Both problems will be solved as soon as you authorise another Starship transport to Garbo. Why have the transports been stopped?"

"I will come to that, but in the meantime, I want the infestation dealt with. Immediately."

"Does this have anything to do with the upcoming elections by any chance?"

"I will ignore that too. But take care, young man." She glowered at him.

"Let me get to the main reason I have summoned you. Your report on the last voyage of the Starship Contaminante. How could they have messed up first contact? They had strict instructions. Tell me what happened."

"Have you not read my report?"

"I am asking the questions here. Yes, I have read your report but I am looking for a deeper dive into this whole affair. A verbal report often throws up new perspectives."

Balthazar was enjoying himself. He felt he had her on the back foot. "Why ask me about this? Why not get a report directly from the captain of the Contaminante?"

"That is not possible."

"Why not?"

"The captain of the Contaminante is dead, along with his crew."

Balthazar's enjoyment morphed into shock. "What? How?"

"The ship blew up, unexpectedly, on its journey back to Earth."

She let this information sink in for a few seconds.

"This is why I feel your perspective on this affair would be invaluable."

Balthazar took a moment to process this information.

"It is simple. The ship received a first contact message from the planet Garbo but an arranged meeting never came to fruition. What more do you need to know?"

"I would like to know how diligently the Contaminante crew searched for the source of the message."

"They scanned the planet and found only what the original survey ships found. No intelligent life forms. The dominant species on the planet is some kind of large ruminant, about twice the size of one of our cows. The creatures can't even talk. All they do is eat grass and erm, 'fertilise' the ground."

"I understand that the volume of 'fertiliser' attracts insects. Is that right?"

"Yes, the captain reported that the planet is infested with trillions of fly-like insects which feed off the ubiquitous manure."

"Yes. But that report came in a month ago. Since then, all our efforts to reestablish contact with the aliens have failed. As you might imagine, our very first contact with an alien civilisation would be a great feather in our cap."

"You mean in your cap."

Analiza ignored him. "In an effort to encourage the aliens, we sent a follow-up ship to do them a great favour. The idea being that by doing so, the aliens would be pleased and reestablish contact."

"And did it work?"

"Yes and no. It did not go quite as expected."

"I don't understand."

"We received this communication earlier today."

Analiza summoned a vid-screen and a large one materialised out of thin air in the middle of the office.

"Play recording," she said.

Balthazar heard a buzzing sound. He noted that it was similar to the buzzing in the original message from the aliens to the captain of the Contaminante.

"Translate message," said Analiza.

The message immediately began again, this time in English.

"This is a message on behalf of the people of the planet Shaturn. Your unprovoked violence toward an innocent family who attempted communication with you was bad enough, but your unprovoked, apocalyptic actions taken against our civilisation was so horrendous that we had no choice but to destroy your ship and report you to the Grand Overlord of the Galaxy. Your species does not deserve to live."

"Shaturn?" queried Balthazar. "I thought the planet was called Garbo."

"Shaturn appears to be the aliens name for their home planet as suggested by the Universal Translator. Their planet has surprisingly elevated levels of excrement. Actually, the Universal Translator offered an alternative name for their planet ... Pooto. We decided to go with Shaturn.

But never mind all that. The problem is that we have no idea what they are talking about. I have brought you here to see if, based on your knowledge of the affair, you have any thoughts."

The blood drained from Balthazar's face.

"What did you do?" he said, accusingly.

"Nothing. We did nothing. We were trying to help them."

"What was the favour you instructed the last starship to grant them?"

"It was instructed to spray their whole planet with insecticide. We thought that by getting rid of the infestation of fly-like insects, they would be pleased."

Balthazar gave her a long hard stare.

"Bring up the original recording of the view through the windscreen of the Contaminante. Stop just before they deploy the screen wipers."

"Why?"

"Humour me."

Analiza gave the instruction. The image froze at the point where the screen was covered in space dust.

"Expand image and stop," he said. The image expanded and the dust became small pebbles.

"Expand again." The image grew until the pebbles could be clearly seen to be not pebbles at all.

"Stop."

Analiza could not believe her eyes. Each 'pebble' now resolved into what looked like an egg, where the tops of the eggs were glass-like helmets. Through the glass she could see small insects all looking forward intently. She thought back to the last part of the original contact recording.

"Their message became incoherent at the end. The universal translator couldn't make sense of it."

Balthazar nodded and whispered, "How do you translate an alien scream?"

* * *

The entity known as the Grand Overlord of the Galaxy expanded and contracted his nebulous body as if it were the chest of some simple, oxygen-breathing life form. The stars within the vast distances of his frameless being moved apart then moved back into place again. He was hyperventilating.

Over limitless periods of time, from his position at the galaxy's centre, he watched over the progress of his galactic community. More often than not, it was not a pretty sight. Many things annoyed him about his subjects. Their constant wars annoyed him, their conflicts between themselves and each other, their greed annoyed him, their general disdain of anyone not like themselves annoyed him. And right now, he was annoyed at constantly being misgendered. Everyone always referred to him as he, when it should be clearly evident to anyone that he was gender neutral. Maybe he should change his title from Overlord to Over … thing? Sometimes language just broke down.

He didn't really care. At this moment, he was feeling every billion of his three billion years. The last half billion years had not been easy and all he wanted now was a holiday. A short period of time with no problems so he could relax, create a few new solar systems, start a few supernovas, enjoy himself. But no. He gets a call from one of his under-overlords. This one happened to be calling from the outer edge of the galaxy, from one of the spiral arms.

"Overlord, this is Underlord 432. I must report a complaint from my sector."

Even from the edge of the galaxy, the Underlord felt an almost imperceptible disturbance in the intra-galactic equilibrium; the Overlord's equivalent of a weary sigh, then heard, "Go ahead 432."

"The complaint concerns a planet called Earth."

"Never heard of it."

"Nor I, till a couple of thousand years ago. It belongs to a system way out on the edge. It's the kind of solar system you would be wise to pass through only in daylight. Definitely not on a dark night. Not even during a total eclipse. Actually, from what I have seen of the people there, I suspect you'd get mugged if you even blinked. It's in the middle of nowhere really, but the point is, this is a serious complaint. These Earth people have been behaving aggressively toward their nearest neighbours. They have dumped their toxic waste on them without their permission and used violence against them on their first meeting."

The Great Overlord of the Galaxy felt the equivalent of a celestial bowel movement and accidentally expelled a globular cluster and a significant volume of dark matter.

"So, nothing good to say about the offending planet. What is the name of the offended planet?"

"They call their planet Shaturn. The Earth people call it Garbo."

"Shaturn?"

"The insectoid inhabitants eat excrement, including their own."

"Ew! To be honest I prefer the Earthmen's name for it. But hey, each to their own. Although I couldn't think of a worse name for a planet."

"You haven't heard the alternative name …"

The Great Overlord of the Galaxy considered the options. To put in a remedial government or make an example of them. He was not in the mood for fact finding and long deliberation, but felt he should at least make a token effort.

"Tell me 432, are there any redeeming features of this … Earth? Morality wise? Culturally?"

Some of the stars on the edges of 432's nebulous brain jiggled involuntarily. The Overlord sensed it.

"You are laughing, 432. Why?"

"Morality wise, absolutely not. They claim a level of morality that is rarely borne out by their actions. Especially their actions toward other life forms. Many creatures on their own planet have become extinct due to their selfish and reckless behaviour. They weren't so bad when they were content merely ruining their own planet, but now they have moved on to wrecking other planets, they have become a problem. However, they perform better culturally. They all watch a regular vid-cast called 'Strictly'. It has been broadcast regularly for over a thousand years."

"What's good about it?"

"As a non-corporeal being, I am perhaps not the best judge, but the humans like it. Human is the name they give to their species."

"What do the humans do in this vid-cast?"

"They jump about a bit. It may be some kind of mating ritual. The Shaturnians have a similar vid-cast. Such activities seem to be favoured by many corporeal species. Actually, I prefer the Shaturnian's version. As an insectoid life form, they have the option of aerial acrobatics. Adds an extra dimension, literally."

"You mean they like to watch themselves mating? That's disgusting."

432 gave an Underlord's equivalent of a shrug, creating a few new comets in the process. "You get used to it."

"Get used to it? How many of these vid-casts have you seen?"

"Not many. I'm only on season 357 of the Earth show and season 152 of the Shaturnian show."

"And what do the Shaturnians call their version of the show?"

"They do their dancing above a lake of slurry. So they call their version of the show, 'Shitly'.

"Shitly? Really?"

"I suspect this may be a poor translation from their language. At least, I hope so."

The Overlord brooded for a moment. "Nothing you have said about these humans warms me to them. I have decided to make an example of them."

432 was shocked. "Surely they will get the regulation second chance?"

"Of course, but from what I have heard from you, these life forms think they are superior to everyone else and any second chance they get will likely be squandered."

432 raised his nebulous eyebrows at the implied superiority of the Overlord's comment but said nothing.

"You disapprove, do you not?"

"I am used to following regulations."

"I sense it is more than that," said the Grand Overlord. "I sense that you have an interest in these Earth people and you are curious about what it would be like to actually be corporeal. If you were corporeal, what would you like to do?"

"A Paso Doble? Wait. I am receiving a new communication." 432 paused to absorb the new message. The tone of his communication became subdued.

"Overlord, you were right. The Shaturnians have been all but wiped out by the Humans. What do you recommend?"

"Up until now, I was merely going to suggest deleting their show 'Strictly' from their race memory, but now ... Clearly, they are an infestation and must be treated as such. Recycle them."

"All of them?"

"Yes. All of them. Are there any recycle centres near their system?"

"The humans call them black holes. There are none nearby. Until now, it has been an uneventful part of the Sector."

"Then create one using their sun."

"O Great Overlord, you are wise. It shall be done. But may I ask one small favour?"

"Name it."

"May I delay this action until I have caught up with all the Strictly episodes?"

"Permission granted."

Fairies: Assemble

"Some fairies say they don't believe humans exist."
Fairy Queen

Fairy Binky glared at the 5-year-old boy across his cluttered bedroom. He glared back, gripping his pillow like the weapon of mass destruction that it was. He gave his dummy a couple of loud sucks in mocking defiance. She was not so easily deterred. She came from a long line of Binkys and the honour of her family was at stake. This was her first solo 'dummy recovery' mission. Failure was not an option.

She hovered by the bedroom door then darted to stand among the toys on his bedside table. She picked up a plastic toy soldier. He swung the pillow around his head then aimed it at her. She leapt into the air just in time. The pillow scattered the table-top toys around the room. She used the distraction to fly behind his head. The boy looked around for her, waving the pillow around randomly, hoping to find his mark. Frustrated, he stamped his feet.

Binky rose above his head then dropped the toy soldier in front of his face. He looked down. She flew under his chin, grabbed the dummy, placed a foot on each side of his mouth then pulled with all her strength. The spittle covered dummy came away easily in her hands. Job done. She headed for the open window with it and was almost through when knocked sideways by a flying pillow. She fell to the carpet, dazed. She needed to get up, quickly, but couldn't move. The last thing she saw before passing out, was the bottom of the child's shoe coming down toward her face.

* * *

When fairy Binky came to, she was lying on the branch of a tree in the arms of fairy Jabby. The leaves of the tree filtered the light from a nearby streetlamp but even so, she squinted.

"What … where am I?" she groaned. Bruised all over, she looked into the face of a concerned Jabby. The lamplight reflected off his hi-vis jacket giving her face a strange, orangey complexion.

"How are you feeling?" he said. "You look a bit pale … and orange."

She felt like something unmentionable but before she could say so, she remembered a huge shoe coming down on her. "How am I still even here? Have I died and gone to the Great Glen?"

"I saved you in the nick of time, and no, this is not the Great Glen. If we were in the Great Glen, it wouldn't be raining."

She realised that she was getting wet. Her pink dress was beginning to stick to her legs.

"Come on, let's get back. Can you fly?"

She nodded. "I think so. But what about the dummy. I can't go back without the dummy."

Fairy Jabby hovered up to a nearby branch and plucked the dummy from the twig where he had placed it.

He grinned at her. She smiled back and rose to join him. Her flight was very wobbly. Jabby told her to stop and she dropped back down to stand on the branch of the tree. The tip of her right wing was bent. Jabby carefully unfolded it until it was back to normal. He took fairy Binky's hand and holding the dummy in his other hand they flew back towards the Dell. When they could see the lights of the Dell in the distance, fairy Binky turned to Jabby. "I can make my own way back from here, thank you."

"No no. You're in no fit state to go alone. I should take you all the way back to your place and help you out of those wet clothes."

She laughed. "That would be very ... interesting, I am sure, but I don't think my parents would approve."

"You live with your parents?"

"Of course." She looked down and pointed towards an area of the Dell. "You can drop me off down there at the end of Columbine Crescent."

"Columbine Crescent? So, you live on the posh side of the Dell. I hear you can see the Queen's palace from there."

"Yes, that's true."

They flew to a large, old oak tree and descended to a low horizontal branch. The branch was long, wide, curved in a crescent shape and dotted with fairy residences. Candlelight from their windows cast a warm glow along the entire branch.

"Which one is yours?" asked Jabby.

"Never you mind. I'll be fine from here." She smiled at him and turned to walk along the branch. "I'll see you tomorrow at work," she shouted back.

Jabby did not move. He called back to her. "Haven't you forgotten something? You'll need this to prove you got the job done." She turned back. He held out the dummy. She flew gracefully back to him to retrieve it, kissed him on the cheek, and with a stern voice, "Now go!"

Jabby began to fly away but he really wanted to see her house. After a few seconds, he turned to look back but fairy Binky had gone.

* * *

The next day found fairy Albert and fairy Clive in the glade, lounging on their favourite mossy log.

Albert was wearing a new hat. He was surprised that Clive had not commented on it. It was one of the trending acorn hats topped with a curly tail. Clive thought it looked ridiculous but decided it would be fun to say the opposite. "Nice hat," said Clive. "It really suits you. Where did you get it? TK Minns?"

Fairy Albert affected a supercilious look. He gazed meaningfully into the distance. "No, I thought I would go upmarket. I got it from Elfridges. They have a new department. Fashions for the older fairy. I feel I have reached a time of life, a certain age, you might say, a measure of maturity, when I should pay more attention to how I look. I feel I need more gravitas. I want people to take me more seriously. Respect the wisdom of my years."

He turned, expecting to see Clive nodding agreement but Clive was no longer sitting next to him. Fairy Clive had fallen off the back of the log and was rolling on the floor laughing.

"Why do I get the feeling you were humouring me?"

Fairy Clive did not get the chance to reply. They were interrupted by the vision that was fairy Hunter flying towards them, legs crossed in her usual lotus position and with hands pressed together. She hovered in front of them while Clive brushed bits of the woodland floor off his orange, hi-vis jacket and got back up onto the log.

Fairy Hunter gave Albert a puzzled look. "There will be a special crisis meeting at The Ring in thirty minutes. Your presence is requested. I expect to see you there shortly." She turned to leave but after a moment turned back, shook her head and spoke again. "Ditch the hat, Albert. You look ridiculous." She then flew off in the direction of The Ring.

"Why does nobody ever take me seriously?" said Albert.

Fairy Clive gave him a hard stare. "Half an hour is not enough time to answer that. Come on, we'd better follow."

Fairy Albert removed his new hat and set it down carefully on the log. He gave a long sigh then rose into the air with Clive and headed toward The Ring.

* * *

The Ring, situated in a small clearing in the woods, was the place where important decisions were made or major news imparted. Lesser news was disseminated via fairy iPads in the usual way. In truth, the area known as The Ring should have been called 'The Rings' because the audience sat on two very large concentric circles of naturally occurring toadstools. Clive always felt this to be a little distasteful. Such a cliché he thought. But when they got to The Ring, they were surprised to find a major change. The centre of The Ring contained a monolithic structure made from silvery metal wires and looked like a giant birdcage. Except that this birdcage had four small wheels attached at the top. One at each corner.

They chose a couple of toadstools set close together on the outer ring and waited for the meeting to begin. As they waited, other fairies were arriving, singly and in groups. They took their places according to seniority, the team leaders, like fairy Hunter, sat in the inner circle. Some of the new arrivals they recognised and some they did not. One fairy they instantly recognised was fairy McFairyFace. He flew in aggressively and dislodged another fairy from his seat. McFairyFace took possession of it. Being manager of the tooth-grinding factory, allowed him a seat on the inner ring.

"If we need to rely on the likes of McFairyFace to get us over a crisis then things must be really bad," said Clive.

Fairies now began arriving in greater numbers. There were representatives of teams Albert and Clive had never seen before. They tended to arrive in twos and threes, the team leaders settling in the inner circle, the workers on the outside.

Albert recognised a young fairy he had seen before. "Isn't that fairy Binky? I think she's really pretty. Don't you think she's pretty?"

"Hmm," replied Clive, noncommittally. "When I look at her, I find myself wondering why a fairy with a name like that is working in tooth grinding. All the Binky's I have ever heard of, worked in dummy recovery or binky recovery, same thing. I don't even know why those human babies have binkies. Or anything for that matter. The last time I checked, human and fairy hands come with handy, built-in pacifiers. They are called thumbs. I still use mine when I have to send in my fairy tax return."

"I heard she was being fast tracked. Somebody wants her to experience every job," said Albert. Albert was about to say something more, when fairy Jabby appeared out of the sky. They expected him to sit behind McFairyFace as he usually worked in tooth grinding. However, he flew straight to fairy Binky and sat beside her.

"Hey!" said Albert, "did you see the way she looked at him? That Jabby, I don't know how he finds the energy. If firkytoodling was a method of social advancement, he would be king by now."

"Firkytoodling *is* a method of advancement," said Clive. "Always has been. But talking about royalty, look who's just arriving."

They squinted into the distance and saw a halo of golden light approaching. "If I didn't know better, I'd say it was the Fairy Queen inside that bubble of light," said Clive.

"It *is* the queen," said Albert, who had better eyesight. "Look, she's holding her golden wand."

The queen, accompanied by two other fairies, flanking her on either side, descended gracefully to stand on top of the metal cage. The general loud chattering became a hushed chattering as the audience realised how important this meeting must be.

The queen at that point was still surrounded by her aura of brightness. The light faded when she drew the end of her golden wand to her and pressed a button on the golden fairy iPad attached to the end of it.

"She has a new wand," observed Albert. "The new one is just a selfie stick with her iPad stuck on the end."

"If you had to update your FairyBook page as often as she does, I think you would do the same," whispered Clive.

The queen was dressed entirely in an outfit of gold topped with a headband made from gold thread. She lowered her selfie stick wand and the assembled fairies gradually became silent. She began to address them.

"Fairy leaders, fairy workers, fairy friends, I greet you all. Sadly, I bring disturbing news. It may come as a surprise to most of you who attend to matters connected with the world of humans on a daily basis, but some fairies don't believe humans exist. However, their existence has become undeniable in recent times. You need look no further than the object I stand upon. This is not of our world. Some of you may recognise it. Can anybody tell me what it is?"

A voice from the outer circle shouted out. "It's an upturned shopping trolley!"

The queen smiled. "Yes, that is correct, fairy …?"

"Fairy Albert," said the voice.

"Thank you, fairy Albert. I see you are a fairy of the world. Sadly, the object I stand upon is not the first to spoil our home. It is one of many, and these objects, not to mention an avalanche of litter, are increasing in number almost daily. An object the size of this is beyond the power of a single fairy to move. Beyond the power of even many fairies working as individuals. However, it should not be beyond the power of all of us, as long as we work together."

The fairy queen paused to scan the fairy faces sitting around her. They looked serious and engaged. She continued to speak, turning slowly to ensure she included everyone sitting behind her.

"The human world is very large. Our world is very small. But every year, the human world encroaches further into ours. They have so much, but seem to care little for it. They take much, they use it, toss it aside then take more. We have little, and the less we have, the more we must cherish it.

Today, I was truly shocked to receive a report from one of my scouts. The waters of the river that flows by the northern borders of The Glen, waters which once ran crystal clear, now run dirty brown. Not a natural brown from mud, but the worst kind of brown. A smelly, putrid brown from human waste. If this wasn't bad enough, my scout saw, floating along in the brown, thousands of dead fish. And what's worse, because of recent storms, the river level is very high and the effluent is beginning to seep into the streams and rivulets of The Glen. The very source of all our drinking water. The source of life for us and for all the creatures who live here. Let this be a warning. Tell everyone you know to be very, very careful where you all get your water.

The humans have done their best to ruin this beautiful woodland world of ours and now it seems they are intent on ruining our streams and our river. Well, I am here to tell you that enough is enough. We say *no more*. We stand our ground. We stop them.

The magnitude of the problem is such that I am proposing we create an elite team of fairies to deal with it. We are looking for fairies who are courageous, capable or who have special skills. The best of the best. Once chosen, they will not be working alone. They will need the support of every other fairy in our land. If we overcome this crisis at all, we shall overcome it together. Any questions?"

McFairyFace spoke up. "Yes. Why are we bothering with the humans at all? Why not just split ourselves off from them? Let their lost teeth and used binkies rot where they fall?"

"Because we both have to share the same world. There is no place on it where they will not find us. That is why we must engage with the humans. We must do it now before matters get worse. Any other questions?"

Fairy Jabby put up his hand.

The queen noticed him. "Yes fairy …? Fairy Jabby, isn't it? I heard about your recent act of bravery. You are to be commended. What is your question?"

"How will the elite fairies be chosen?"

"A good question. Your team leaders have been briefed and will explain. Thank you for your attention. Now, I must leave you. Fairies forever!" She pressed a button on her iPad and, surrounded by a bubble golden light, rose into the air with her acolytes and disappeared into the sky.

* * *

On their way back from the meeting, fairy Albert and fairy Clive decided to rest in the middle of a moss-covered bridge over a slow-moving stream. Their legs dangled over the edge and they both gazed down into the tranquil waters below them.

Clive noted Albert's glum face reflected in the water. "What's up?"

"It's that Jabby. How does he do it? He and fairy Binky seem to be an item already. It sometimes seems like everyone is firkytoodling except me. Not with a girl anyway."

"Too much information," said Clive.

Albert continued to whine. "I haven't had a date for as long as I can remember. Fairy Binky doesn't give me a second glance."

Clive regarded Albert carefully. Sat next to him, Albert was a study in gloom. He would be positive.

"You *can* have a relationship. Anyone can. You just have to work at it. Put some effort in. You know what they say, faint heart never won fair fairy."

"No. It's no use. There's no hope for me."

"Come on my old friend, there's always hope. Nobody is that irredeemable. As I said, you just need to put a bit of effort into it. Let me see, if I were to ask you right now, is there any girl, other than Binky, that you fancy?"

"Of course there is."

"Who?"

Albert's face suddenly lit up. "She's called Victoria. She's a pop singer. Pretty famous too."

"Fairy Victoria? Never heard of her. But what I meant is, who do you fancy in the real world? Not some unreachable pop star in your dream world."

Albert's face darkened again. "So what you're saying is, for any firkytoodling to come my way, it can only happen in some kind of dream or fantasy world?"

"Yes. I mean no. Let me think. Maybe we need to look at this from a different angle … Okay. You must have had a girlfriend in the past."

Albert's face changed from glum to glummer. "I don't want to talk about that. It didn't go well."

"You have to. If we are to learn from the past then we must confront it. Tell me all about it and maybe I can advise you how to go forward."

Albert sighed. "I went on a dating site called Fairy Match.com a few years ago and met this really nice girl. It was all going well until she said she wanted to kiss me."

"How could *that* possibly go wrong?"

"Well, when she came at me, her kissing sucked."

Clive frowned. "I don't understand."

"I mean, she put her mouth around mine, opened it with her tongue and then sucked. She sucked like one of those vacuum cleaners the humans are so fond of."

"That doesn't sound too bad," said Clive. "What was the problem? Afraid she was going to suck the breath out of you?"

"No. That bit was alright. The problem was when she sucked out one of my fillings and choked on it."

"Ouch," said a startled Clive. "Okay so your first meeting didn't go well, but did she want to see you again?"

"She did, but I told her I couldn't afford the dentist bills."

"You know Albert, I have changed my mind. There *is* no hope for you."

Albert stared back down into the reflective waters, seemingly lost in thought. Clive noticed Albert's rare moment of introspection. He wondered what Albert was thinking and turned to speak to him.

"What do you see when you look down at yourself?"

Clive had to wait a full 15 seconds before a reply was forthcoming.

"I see a fish," said Albert.

"A fish? That's interesting. Do you see yourself as a shark? A salmon? What kind of a fish?"

"A dead one."

"You see yourself as a dead fish? I wasn't expecting that."

"No. Look down. I see a dead fish floating by. And the water is muddy."

Clive looked down and indeed there was a large dead fish floating under the bridge in a mass of sludgy, cloudy water. He sniffed the air.

"That's not mud in the water."

"What do you think it is?"

"I don't want to know but it looks a lot like what the Fairy Queen was talking about. And smells like it."

In silence, they watched several dead fish float by before flying home. On the way back, Albert had an idea.

"I know what I need to do to impress Binky. What we both should do. We could do what the fairy Queen says. Become 'Elite' fairies. The best of the best. Part of a crack team doing good in the world!"

Now it was Clive's turn to be negative.

"Crack team? Elite fairies? We're just tooth fairies. Why would they choose us? And doing good? Really? We visit these kids. We take their teeth. We give them money, and what do they do with it? They use it to buy sweets! I don't know that we are actually doing any good in this world at all."

"Well I disagree," said Albert. "We work hard at annoying fairy McFairyFace don't we? That's doing good in the world."

Clive reluctantly agreed. "Yes, I suppose so. That's good and it's enjoyable, but there's only so much of that we can do."

They had arrived back at their mossy log. Albert's hat was still where he left it. He had just put it back on when he saw three fairies approaching from the direction of the tree canopy above the pool by their home. When he realised that it was fairy Hunter flanked by Jabby and fairy Binky, Albert removed his hat and dropped it behind the log.

"Greetings," said fairy Hunter. "I believe you already know fairy Jabby and fairy Binky."

Albert and Clive nodded.

"I know that under normal circumstances, missions call for a maximum of two agents but this one requires extra backup. Jabby can fill you in on the details but basically, fairy Binky went on a mission yesterday to recover a dummy. She came back with Jabby."

Albert and Clive both raised eyebrows. She clarified her statement. "Erm, and the dummy, of course. But today we have had an email from the parents saying their child has another dummy. He refuses to part with it and they need our help. I should warn you that the child's father says that he is an MP (whatever that is) and is not used to getting bad service like this. Says that if we do not get our act together, there will be consequences."

"What consequences?" said Albert.

"He doesn't say. However, due to unforeseen circumstances yesterday and this email I am sending you and Clive with Binky and Jabby as backup."

"Unforeseen circumstances?" queried Clive.

"Let's just say that the level of child resistance in this case was underestimated."

Albert and Clive exchanged nervous glances. Fairy Hunter continued.

"The mission is still fairy Binky's. And one more thing, bearing in mind that our queen was talking about choosing fairies for an elite team, this mission will be scrutinised. So …" She looked at Albert and Clive. "… I know you two are my best agents, but you won't get onto the team by default. You have to do something worthy. Just … be the best you can be. I know you can do it. Be the best. Be worthy. Good luck."

With this, she flew off, maintaining a perfect lotus position the whole time.

"She's impressive," said fairy Binky. She copied fairy Hunter's flying method and slowly wobbled into the air.

Jabby wasn't impressed. "It's easy. I'll show you how it's done." He attempted to copy fairy Hunter and immediately crashed into the side of a tree.

Albert and Clive ignored him. "Be worthy?" said Albert. "I can be worthy … I think." He screwed up his face and looked at Clive.

"This is my best 'worthy face', what do you think?"

"Looks more like your 'constipated face'," said Clive.

Once Jabby recovered from his tree encounter, fairy Binky related the whole story of her first solo mission.

"If it was a solo mission then what was Jabby doing there?" asked Albert.

It was the first-time fairy Binky thought about it. "Yes Jabby, why *were* you there? Didn't they trust me?"

"I'm not allowed to say. It seems that somebody wanted you to have a guardian fairy. Lucky they did, as it turns out."

"Ok," said Albert, grabbing his hat, "we'd better go to the grotto and stock up on fairy dust before we set off."

"Wait a minute," said fairy Binky, "I'm in charge here."

"Sorry," said Albert. "What do you want us to do?"

"I think we should all go to the grotto and stock up on fairy dust."

* * *

At the grotto, they were met by fairy McFairyFace at the reception desk. He considered his purpose in life was to do as little as possible and generally prevent fairy folk from obtaining the dust they needed. Today he seemed grumpier than usual.

"What's up?" asked Clive, "you had to do some real work for once?"

"I haven't got time to deal with this. Our dust production quota has just doubled and we're short staffed." He glared at Jabby who normally manned the fairy dust counter. "And now we have to provide dust to time wasters like you. Why it takes four of you to retrieve one dummy off a toddler I'll never know. 'Pinky' Binky should be able to do that with one wing tied behind her back. All you tooth fairies are the same. Firkytoodling every chance you get. So, no firkytoodling. Just get what you need and then firk off!"

They passed through to the dust distribution counter.

"Charming," said Albert. "Why did he call you 'Pinky' Binky?"

"He teases me because I always wear pink."

A fairy they had not met before, the largest fairy they had ever seen, manned the dust counter. "Prynhawn da," he said. "I'm fairy Ted, but everyone calls me Chubbs. Pleased to meet you."

"Prynhawn da?" queried Albert. "What does that mean?"

"It means good afternoon in Welsh."

"I thought you didn't sound local," said Albert.

"I'm not. I'm an immigrant. We have several immigrants working here now, what with the crisis and everything. What do you need?"

"Four bags of dust please, and two extra shoulder bags, one for Jabby and one for fairy Binky."

Fairy Chubbs fetched four bags from under the counter and placed them on top. He looked around for some shoulder bags but could see none.

"Up there on the top shelf," said Jabby, who knew the place intimately.

Fairy Chubbs sighed. He beat his wings together strenuously but rose only a few inches into the air. He tried again but fared even worse. His wings weren't strong enough to lift his weight.

"No problem," said Jabby, "I've got this." He flew up to the top shelf in a matter of seconds to grab a couple of shoulder bags.

Albert noticed fairy Binky giving Jabby an admiring glance. As they were leaving, Albert was thinking. Clive noticed Albert thinking and was concerned for him.

"I never thought I would ever hear myself saying this, but I kind of agree with McFairyFace," said Albert. "Why *isn't* this a one-fairy job? Most dummy recovery missions are easy. Like taking candy off a baby. Literally."

"This is no baby," explained Jabby, "this kid is a five-year-old terrorist. And on top of that, he's vicious."

"Five years old!" exclaimed Clive. "What are his parents thinking about? A normal dummy extraction happens between the ages of one or two."

"Age five is nothing," said fairy Binky, "my nanny said her uncle worked in dummy recovery for years. He told her he was sent to an eleven-year-old once."

"You had a nanny!?" exclaimed Albert.

"She lives on the *posh* side of the Dell," explained Jabby.

Fairy Binky looked nervous.

"Don't look so worried," said Albert as they all took to the air and headed off on their mission. "We can do this. "They told us to be the best, but we really are the best. Isn't that right Clive?"

Clive picked up on Albert's concern for fairy Binky. "No question about it." He started to hum a tune to himself as they flew through the darkening woodland.

"Uh oh," said Albert. "I sense a song coming on."

"A song?" queried fairy Binky. Albert nodded as Clive slowed down and then stopped in mid-air. The others stopped too then Clive began an aerial dance and started to sing.

We're the Best

We're the best
We're the best
Put our courage to the test
You won't fail to be impressed, you see
We never get depressed
We are great
We can't wait
Facing danger is our fate

As we go to grab a binky
Off a baby not so dinky
We don't stop
We don't rest
We go north ... south, east and west
We are fighting for the bullied and oppressed
And when we flex our wings
We can do anything
We're the best
We're the Best
We're the best

At this point, Albert and Jabby decided to enter the aerial display, joining in with the chorus. The three of them performed a mid-air ballet, making acrobatic loops and contortions. When a yellow butterfly crossed their path, they each danced around it before letting it go on its way. Meanwhile, fairy Binky sat on the low branch of a nearby tree from which to watch their antics.

We're the new
Fairy crew
There is nothing we can't do
We even dare to fight a bear
I know, it's crazy, but it's true
We care more
Never less
We save damsels in distress
No, we don't know mathematics
But we can do acrobatics
We are cool
We've no fear
It won't take us long to clear

All the evils that infest this fairy world
How is it we can do
The things we have to do
We're the best
We're the best
We're the best

Their display was taking place only a few metres above the ground. From the corner of his eye, Clive saw movement below. "Pixie!" he shouted. The pixie, half hidden between the stems of some bramble, had a catapult and was about to fire. Clive's warning came too late. The pixie's ammunition, a juicy blackberry, hit Albert full in the face. The three fairies flew to a nearby hazel tree and rained hazelnuts down on the pixie until he ran off. The three of them cheered and went back to their aerial antics.

We're the best
We're the best
And we don't say that in jest
We will challenge any beast you see
And deal with any pest
Don't you say
We are small
Please don't mention that at all
We admit that we are teeny
But we're never ever weeny
We are drab
Not ritzy
And though we may be itsy-bitsy
We can tame a tricksy pixie
And if you ever plan to see
A flight of fairy fantasy

We're the best
We're the best
We're the best

As Clive completed his performance, they attempted one last spectacular aerial manoeuvre. Sadly, it was a spectacular failure as the three fairies smashed into each other and fell to the ground in a tangle of arms, legs and wings. They lay there looking up at fairy Binky.

"We're the best!" they all shouted together.

Fairy Binky looked down on the pile of bodies below pitifully. "If you're the best, I'm not impressed," she said, smiling.

When they were back in the air beside her, fairy Binky had a question for Albert, who was attempting to wipe the blackberry juice off his face. "Is Clive always like this?" she asked.

"No," said a purple faced Albert, "usually he's a lot worse."

Fairies: Endgame

Once in the bedroom of the dummy monster, the four fearless fairies found him sleeping.

"That's lucky", said Binky. "All we need to do now is find that dummy."

They scanned the bedroom. The child was asleep on a bed in the corner. Otherwise, the room was a complete mess.

"Do you think this house has just been burgled?" asked Albert.

Jabby lifted some bedding covering random toys on the floor. One of them was a robot. It sparked into life the second it was freed. The robot began walking toward them in robotic fashion and with a loud grinding of metallic gears and a red light on top of its head flashing ominously.

"Look," said Binky, "it has a dummy in its mouth!"

She flew down to grab it but it was difficult to dislodge and while she engaged with it two more robotic toys appeared to self-activate. These were both T-Rexes with chomping jaws. They too began marching toward her in a threatening manner.

Jabby and Albert dived down and knocked the T-Rexes over and while they were doing so the child leapt out of his bed and grabbed them.

"Get off my robot, or else!" he shouted, threateningly.

"Or else what?" said Clive.

"Or else I'll tell my dad on you. And he is an MP."

"What's an MP?" said Clive.

The child frowned. "I don't know but he is very powerful."

"Go on then. I don't care how strong he is because I don't think your dad will care. He's the one who called us in to start with."

The exultant look on the boy's face melted away. Clive assumed he had won the argument, but the child grinned.

"He will when he finds out you're hurting me."

"We're not hurting you." Clive looked at Albert and Jabby dangling upside down, their legs, still in the child's firm grip. "You are hurting *us* if anything. Why don't you put my friends down and we'll talk?"

In a matter of seconds, the child's grin morphed into a look of utter pain. He dropped Albert and Jabby and began crying his eyes out and wailing as loud as he could. This was followed by the sound of footsteps coming up the stairs at a rapid pace. Albert and Jabby scrambled to their feet. Meeting an adult human was a big no-no. Even to be seen by one was forbidden. They must do everything possible to avoid contact. This had been fairy lore from the beginning of time. Albert flew up to hover next to Clive and Jabby dashed to help Binky dislodge the dummy from the robot's jaws. They then flew with the dummy to hover next to the others but before they could decide what to do next, the bedroom door flung open and the child's father entered. The four fairies hid behind it.

"Tarquin? What on earth's the matter?" he shouted.

Tarquin blubbered something about evil fairies.

"Now, now, calm down. You must have had a bad dream." He was about to say there was no such thing as fairies but that would ruin the tooth fairy tale. "Fairies are invisible. Nobody has ever seen a tooth fairy. They come at night and only while you are sleeping."

"But there is fairies," squealed Tarquin, ungrammatically. "There they is! Behind the door. One of them is wearing a silly acorn hat." He pointed to the bedroom door.

To humour him, his father grabbed the door handle and closed the door without looking behind it.

"You see, there's nothing there."

But Tarquin's extended arm continued to point towards the door.

His father at last turned around, stared at the four hovering fairies and gasped.

"But, but, but you don't exist," he stuttered.

"But, but, but we do," said Clive, who felt he should take command of the situation, seeing himself to be the only one with any sense.

"What are you doing here?" said Tarquin's father.

"We are doing, or attempting to do what you asked us to do and remove Tarquin's dummy. Just as we did with his last one."

"Yes, but I never thought … I never thought real fairies would do it. I thought the App was a joke."

"Then who did you think was actually dealing with baby teeth and dummies?"

"My wife."

"Did she confess to it?"

"No, she denied it, but I assumed she was lying."

"Why would you think she would lie to you?"

"Because in my line of work people lie all the time."

"And you don't even trust your own wife?"

The human looked around then in a lower voice, "Especially not my own wife. And why should I believe anything you lot say? One of you already looks red faced. Well, more purple faced really."

"That's Albert," said Clive. "He was hit in the face with a blackberry by a pixie with a catapult."

Reflecting on what he had just said, Clive realised this conversation was getting them nowhere.

"But never mind all that. The point is that your child is wayward. Totally unmanageable. In the old days a kid would have been given a colouring book and some crayons. Now they have robots."

Suddenly Clive was hit on the head with a flying crayon. "Ow!"

Clive nodded to Jabby. "Time for some dust I think."

Jabby returned the nod, confirming he understood the instruction and grinned. He flew over Tarquin's head, grabbed a handful of fairy dust from his bag and sprinkled it over the boy's head. "Sleep and forget," he said. Tarquin immediately fell asleep.

"What have you done?" exclaimed the father.

"He was being a nuisance. He's asleep now."

The angry dad looked like he was about to make an indignant response but after a moment's thought, appeared to change his mind and said, "Can I have a bag of that?"

Clive ignored him.

"Your son tells me you are a man of power and influence in the human world. An … MP?"

The father nodded.

"And what exactly is an MP?"

"An MP is a very important person."

"So I hear, but what does an MP do?"

The MP frowned. "Well, lots of things. I go to meetings. I make speeches. Lots of things."

Fairy Clive gave him a hard stare. "Yes, but what do you do that's actually useful?"

The MP frowned harder and appeared to be struggling to find a response. Having thought of something he smiled.

"An MP makes laws and sorts out people's problems. He makes their lives better."

"That sounds good. To enable me to understand fully, perhaps you could give me two or three examples of how you have made lives better."

The MP frowned again and looked annoyed. "Look, I can't think of anything right now. These things take time, but there are loads of examples. Ask anybody in my constituency."

"Constituency? What's that?"

"It means the people who live around here. If anybody has a problem, I can fix it."

"That's good," said Clive, "because we live around here and we have a problem."

"Oh?"

"Our river and waterways are polluted. What are you going to do about it?"

"I can't help with that. That's a sewage plant problem."

"So, you can't fix people's problems after all."

"Well, there would have to be new legislation to make it illegal."

"And how long will that take?"

"Months, maybe years."

"But in the meantime, we have no fresh water to drink," complained Binky.

"These things take time."

"We don't have time."

"There's nothing I can do."

Clive's frustration now boiled over. He turned to Jabby. "You see that glass of water on the bedside table Jabby?" Jabby nodded. "Put a pinch or two of dust into it."

Jabby did not know what Clive had in mind this time, but played along. Once the dust was added, the water became cloudy.

"Extend river water pollution to all water in this constituency," said Clive, authoritatively.

The MP's supercilious expression changed to one of panic. "What have you done?"

"All the water in all the houses around here will now be polluted to the same extent as the river until it is cleaned up."

"You can't do that!"

"I just did. How long do you think it will take to sort the problem now?"

The MP went pale. "What am I going to do?"

"You say you are a man of power and influence. Now is the time to prove it."

Clive turned to the others. "Come on everyone. Grab that dummy Binky and let's get out of here."

And with this, the fairy crew rose into the air and left the house through an open window. When they had been flying for about five minutes, Albert could contain himself no longer.

"Clive, what have you done? One… talking to humans is forbidden. And two… what were you thinking back there? Fairy dust can't pollute water!"

"You know that. I know that. But that human? He doesn't appear to know anything."

* * *

The next day Clive was summoned to a private meeting with Fairy Hunter. He was not looking forward to it and told himself that no matter how bad the reprimand for talking to humans, he was going to stand his ground. He confidently marched into her office ready to defend himself.

"I know I shouldn't have done it," he announced, "and I would do the same again in similar circumstances."

Fairy Hunter gave him a strange look and said, "What are you talking about?"

"I'm talking about…" Clive stopped as soon as he realised he had misunderstood the situation. "Nothing. Why did you want to see me?"

"I am here at the special request of the Fairy Queen. What did you think I wanted?"

"Nothing."

She gave him a suspicious look and handed him a large rolled up leaf.

"This is a royal scroll with her request. Read it and let me know if this is something you can handle."

Clive unrolled the leaf, read the fine script, nodded affirmatively and handed the scroll back.

"Thankyou," said Ms hunter. "I look forward to receiving your effort soon."

"You'll have it tomorrow," said Clive as he left.

* * *

Three days later, Albert, Clive and Jabby each received an invite to a Grand Ball at the Fairy Queen's palace. The invitation stated that there would be a short ceremony. There would be food. There would be drink. And there would be entertainment.

"Entertainment!" said an excited Albert. "I wonder what kind of entertainment?"

"I heard there will be a girl band," said Jabby, equally excited. "I heard a rumour that it will be that new group who call themselves the Spice Fairies! I can't wait."

"Never heard of them," said Clive, unimpressed.

"I have," said Albert, beaming because he knew something Clive did not.

Now it was Jabby's turn to be unimpressed. Unimpressed with Clive. "How can you not have heard of the Spice Fairies? Their lead singer is called Mary."

"What?" said Clive. "Fairy Mary?"

"No. The cool thing is that they reverse normal naming. So she calls herself Mary Fairy. The other girls in the band do the same thing."

"And what do they call themselves?"

"There's Airy Fairy, Scary Fairy and Hairy Fairy."

"Airy Fairy is my favourite," said Albert.

"O… kay," said a bemused Clive. "Scary Fairy sounds self-explanatory but why Hairy Fairy?"

"She has this amazing head of big hair," explained Jabby. But never mind all that. We need to get ready. The big do is tonight."

* * *

Before the three of them set off for the palace, Jabby explained that practically every fairy they knew had been invited. Albert decided to wear his acorn hat.

On arrival everyone was sitting in the grand palatial ballroom. A stage had been erected at the front and seating set out in semi-circular fashion. The Fairy Queen sat on her golden mushroom on the stage and the room was packed out with chattering fairies.

"Uh oh," said Albert, "we're late." He scanned the room and saw there were only three unoccupied seats available. All on the front row.

"I hate sitting at the front," said Albert.

"Come on," said Jabby, "we have no choice.

As the three fairies took their seats, the chattering stopped and the room erupted in applause. The late three looked at each other with bemused expressions. The Fairy Queen rose from her mushroom, gestured the audience to quiet themselves and addressed the crowd.

"Fairy leaders, fairy workers, fairy friends, I greet you all. And this time I have good news. Great news."

She gestured to some fairies hiding in the wings. They emerged carrying trays of drinks and began distributing them to the audience. When everyone had a drink, she addressed them again.

"I give you… water! Clean water! Our river is now clear of pollution. And we all have three heroic fairies to thank for it. Fairy Albert, fairy Clive, and fairy Jabby. Please come up onto the stage."

"What's going on?" whispered Albert.

"No idea," said Clive, as they flew up on stage to stand before the Fairy Queen.

She raised her cup. "I propose a toast. To three of the bravest fairies in the Glen."

The crowd immediately jumped to their feet and raised their cups.

"To Albert, Clive and Jabby!" they shouted.

Once the excitement died down, Clive asked the Queen what they were supposed to have done.

"You don't know? Well, it appears that you had a forbidden…" She gave him a disapproving look at the mention of the word 'forbidden'. "A forbidden conversation with a human a few days ago and erm, persuaded him to sort out our water problem."

"Oh, that was nothing really," said Clive modestly. "He seemed to be a human of influence and I just appealed to his better nature."

"Better nature? The man was a politician!" scoffed the Queen. "You are too modest. And we are all here today to celebrate your achievement. In your honour we have created a new award of merit and you shall each receive one in a moment."

At this point, Jabby, who had been holding his tongue, decided he could no longer remain silent.

"Excuse me, your majesty, but there were four of us on that mission and I would not be comfortable accepting this honour if our fourth member was left out."

The Queen gave Jabby a penetrating stare. "That is a very commendable attitude fairy Jabby. I will see that something is worked out. In the meantime,…" She made a gesture to someone off stage. "Please bring on the awards."

To their great amazement, from the stage wings appeared fairy Binky carrying a tray with three boxes made out of long, woven grass.

"The awards will be given," said the Queen, "by my daughter, whom you may know as Princess Binky."

Princess Binky was hardly recognisable in her royal dress made from silver and gold thread. She stood in front of the three fairies, who stared at her open-mouthed, and grinned at them. She placed her tray on a waist high table, opened the first box and took out the award. It was a golden version of the acorn hat which Albert was still wearing. Binky approached him first and smiled at him.

"If you want to put this on, you'd better take off the old one!"

Albert quickly removed it and donned the new one.

"Well done, Albert," she said, and to his utter joy, kissed him on the cheek. She moved onto Clive who groaned inwardly when he saw the hat.

"Well done, Clive," she said, passing him a golden hat and also kissing him on the cheek before moving on to Jabby.

"Well done, Jabby," she said, passing another hat. To Albert's dismay, she kissed Jabby on both cheeks and to roars of approval from the audience.

The queen waited for the applause to die down then introduced the evening's entertainment.

"Please welcome to the stage, the phenomenal supergroup you all know as The Spice Fairies! To begin their concert, they are going to perform a new song, specially commissioned by myself for this occasion. It's a rather beautiful song called Over the Great Glen and it is a message to our human neighbours. I hope you love it as much as I do."

Musicians began to play. The Spice Fairies flew onto the stage by way of choreographed aerial acrobatics and began to sing.

Over the Great Glen

Somewhere over the Great Glen
Fairies fly
We fly down in the dark wood
High in the summer sky

Somewhere inside the Great Glen
Come what may
There's a home where we all live
Work, love and laugh and play

Each day we fly up in the clouds
And look down on the human crowds around us
They spoil our rivers, cut down trees
Build roads and houses as they please
Till they surround us

Somewhere inside the Great Glen
One thing's true
Fairies want to be safe so
Why oh why don't you

If tiny fairy folk like us
Can live our lives without a fuss
Then why oh why can't you

When the song was over, Fairy Hunter made a point of approaching Clive when he was on his own.

"The Fairy Queen was very pleased with your song fairy Clive. She told me to say well done. You never know, keep this up and you may become the royal songwriter!"

* * *

During the party that followed the concert, the water was somehow replaced by something a little stronger. The distinctive taste of the heady fairy brew known as honeydew. Fairies danced disco-style all around and the music throbbed, while Albert and Clive looked on from a table at the perimeter.

Amid all the celebrations however, Albert continued to look resolutely downbeat.

"What's the matter?" asked Clive, "mass adulation, free honeydew and approval by the Fairy Queen not enough for you?"

"It's that Jabby again. Look at him, dancing with Princess Binky."

Clive sighed. He would have to do something. "Oh, do snap out of it. Why don't you go and get us some more drinks?"

While Albert was off getting drinks, Clive wandered onto the dance floor to interrupt Jabby and Binky and ask for their help with the Albert problem. He returned to his table just before Albert arrived with drinks.

"What would need to happen to pull you out of your mood?" said Clive.

Albert's head was down. "I don't want to get out of my mood. I'm trying to get into my fantasy world where I meet Victoria and there's lots of firkytoodling." As Albert was saying this, he looked up at Clive and over his shoulder saw a group of girls approaching their table; Jabby and Binky following close behind. He could not believe his eyes.

"Victoria!"

"Hi Albert."

"But… but… how did you know my name?"

"For one thing, you're famous and also, the golden acorn hat kind of confirms it. Look, I wanted to introduce my fellow

Spice Fairies." She ushered them forward and they embraced Albert in turn as their names were called.

"Mary Fairy, Scary Fairy and Hairy Fairy." Albert lost his face momentarily in a mass of black hair at the last intro.

Clive was puzzled. "Where's Airy Fairy?"

"I'm Airy Fairy," said Victoria. "That's just my stage name, not my real name. Look, the girls have brought their acorn hats for you to autograph."

"Acorn hats?" queried Clive. "Where did you get them?"

"From the side room over there. They are selling them. Everyone's wearing them. They are calling them Albert hats."

"I really must be living in some kind of fantasy world," said Albert. He cast a suspicious glance at Jabby and Binky. "Are you two responsible for this meeting?"

They shook their heads. "It wasn't our idea."

"No," agreed Victoria, "I wanted to meet you. You're more famous than we are right now. And you're a fashion icon."

"You wanted to meet him!?" said Clive. "Now even I must be living in a fantasy world. Maybe we're all living in a fantasy world…"

Old Friends

Albert and Clive sat beside each other on a smart and substantial wooden bench staring at a bed of roses. A warm breeze carried the rich rose perfume in their direction. The sky was blue and the early summer sun lit up the back of Clive's head, glinting off his thinning white hair and revealing his lined face to be a mask of misery. A look which Albert noted seemed to have become Clive's default expression these days.

"So how are you liking it here at the Dead Happy Care Home?"

Clive gave him a hard stare. "If that was supposed to be a joke then you are not far off the mark. There were two funerals here last week. But to answer your question, I do not feel comfortable amongst the pop-cloggers community."

"I thought you would like it here once you got to know who's who and what's what."

"Well, I don't. And these days, not only do you need to know what's what and who's who, you also need to know who's what."

"At least it's not permanent. You'll be home as soon as you're well enough."

Albert rootled around in a bag he had brought with him, took out a gift-wrapped package and handed it to Clive.

"This might cheer you up. Happy 65th birthday," he said.

"What?" moaned Clive. "I don't need cheering up when I am enjoying a good grump and I certainly don't need any more birthdays."

"Well, I beg to differ," said Albert. "I read somewhere that birthdays are good for you. All the statistics confirm that the people who have the most birthdays live the longest."

Clive turned to give Albert another hard stare.

"There is nothing good about growing old. Especially when I am stuck in this care home. And if you're going to throw quotes at me, then I read somewhere that life is like a roll of toilet paper. The closer you get to the end, the faster it goes."

"Okay, okay I give up," said Albert. "No more being nice to you, but aren't you going to open the present?"

Clive squeezed the package resting on his knee. The wrapping paper crinkled.

"What is it?"

Albert grinned. "Open it and you'll see."

Clive ripped the parcel open and revealed something orange. The summer sun reflected off it casting an orange glow upon their faces. He recognised the item immediately.

"A hi-vis jacket!"

"I thought you might like to wallow in a bit of nostalgia for the old days. So happy birthday again."

Clive's grump face softened perceptibly.

"Thank you. But what's there to be happy about being 65? You know, when I was 59, I said to myself, I'm sure my 60s will be fine!

At ages 60 and 61: See. I'm fine!

Ages 62 and 63: Still doing fine!

Then last year, age 64: Suddenly I need various organs removed, I need to know the precise location of all the public toilets in town, 15 foods I eat are causing me heartburn, I can no longer read without glasses, I struggle to breathe even though I never smoked in my life, dairy products hate me and my left knee now predicts rain."

"Yes, but apart from all that you're okay. Remember what you would always say in situations like this? Things could always be worse. It's just your birthday. Get over it and let's go to lunch. I understand that the catering staff here are cooking a special meal. I know you still like your food."

With a begrudging nod, Clive donned his hi-vis jacket and carefully moved from the bench to his wheelchair. As Albert pushed him to the dining room, Clive actually began to reminisce.

"Thirty years ago, we didn't have a dining room. Remember when we were eating bin-baguettes made by Joe at his skip Café? Can't believe he actually lived in that skip for months!"

Albert smiled. "Yeah, and Jabby making rude pictures in the froth on the cappuccinos!"

"Those were the days," said Clive, with a sigh. "When we would sit at our table at Café Joe's and watch the customers deliver up their trash for an hour."

"Really?" said Albert. "You have just been looking at a literal rose garden, but you prefer the ambience of a recycle centre? Plus, you are much happier than I thought you would be to be wearing a hi-vis jacket again. Come on, there's our table. The one with the balloons."

Clive groaned.

* * *

After the other care home diners and staff sang Happy Birthday and made Clive feel even worse, a robo-waiter came to their table to take their order. Clive groaned again.

"And I'll never get used to robot staff. They are everywhere these days. Why can't we have human waiters like in the old days?"

"Robots are cheaper," said the robot. "And less prone to rudeness. May I interest you with some wine to accompany your meal?" The robot handed Clive the wine list.

To Clive, the robot's expressionless face seemed to be a cover for subtle but intentional sarcasm.

"What would you recommend?" he said. "A glass of 3 in One?"

The robot ignored the comment and pointed to the menu.

"Let me see," said the robot. "Your friend seems to be a rather discerning individual. For him I would suggest the Pinot Grigio. An engaging wine, harmonious and persistent with an aroma of…" The robot paused a moment, "… early vapes. The wine teeters on the edge of sweetness but doesn't fall."

"And what would you recommend for me?" said Clive.

"For you sir, I would recommend the Cabernet Sauvignon. An awkward little wine with the texture of old socks and Y-fronts, peppered with pencil shavings. I think sir would appreciate its unique aroma of old tennis balls."

Clive nodded; said, "Sounds delicious," and the robot left.

"If we must have robots, do they all have to be so rude?"

"They are never rude to me," said Albert. "Anyway, you are always complaining about something these days. Look, it can't be all doom and gloom here. Didn't you have some therapy to help with your breathing the other day?"

"Yes. They bus me out to a village hall on the other side of Dedbury. There's me and five others with breathing problems. We all have to meet twice a week for 6 weeks. I call it Breath Club. They make you do exercises and well, you won't believe it but they force you to breathe. Then you have to listen to a variety of encouragement talks. Actually, I can cope with the exercises, it's the talks that get me."

"What do you mean?"

Robo-waiter returned to their table, set two glasses of wine down and left. Clive raised his glass, sniffed it for old tennis balls then drank a mouthful.

"I mean, the last talk was about death. You know, make sure you all make a will etc. Apparently, the NHS would also like people to write down their wishes, should the worst happen."

"What do you mean?"

"Say I end up in hospital for whatever reason and say I can't talk for example and they can't contact relatives. How do the doctors and nurses know how to treat me? Say they were feeding me and they didn't know I was vegetarian or say I was Jewish and had to eat kosher. How could they tell?"

Albert gave Clive a knowing stare.

"Okay, so forget the Jewish example, but you know what I mean. Anyway, the nurse asks has anyone any other examples and one of my fellow Breath Club members reveals that he told his doctor that he wants to be flagged as DNR, 'do not resuscitate'. It was sad. Everyone felt so sorry for him that the guy felt his life was so bad that he didn't want anyone to even attempt keeping him alive. The poor guy went into detail about how restricted his life was and listed a load of other conditions he was suffering with. But, after he'd been talking about it for ten minutes, the nurse could see that some of the other attendees were beginning to look depressed too. She tried changing the subject several times but the guy just kept going. He was still talking about wanting to die when the session was supposed to have finished. The lady next to me started to cry. I tried to comfort her by saying I know, it's so sad, but she whispered that she was upset because she was going to miss her bus. Now, I know what I am about to say is terrible, and I hope you don't think I'm a bad person, but when the guy finally stopped talking, after a full half hour, even I wanted the guy to be flagged as 'do not resuscitate'."

At this point the food was delivered to their table. Albert used the moment to change the subject.

"I went to see Jabby the other day at the recycle centre."

"Oh? How is he?"

"He's the manager there now but he's not happy. Not really. The workers are all robots now. But what's worse for Jabby is that the customers are mainly robots too. Why go to the dump when you can send your robot? The robots call him Lord of the Bins, you know."

Clive laughed. "One bin to rule them all. One bin to find them. One bin to bring them all, and in the darkness bind them. But I don't understand. So why is he unhappy?"

"No good-looking ladies to erm, help."

* * *

After the meal they moved to a picture window overlooking the garden to have coffee. Albert sat in a comfy chair while Clive stayed in his wheelchair.

Clive sipped his coffee and turned to Albert.

"So how is your own health? You're 10 years older than me. I don't know how you keep everything working so well."

"I have my twinges but get by with a little help from Victoria."

"How is she?"

"She's fine. She has a hobby now. She collects pill boxes and pill organisers. The first ones were invented in 1966 in America, you know. And I know what you're thinking. You're thinking our lives don't sound very exciting. But you'd be wrong. We're living on the edge now. They say people stop taking risks in their 70s but we just started a new jigsaw puzzle! And we started it the day before our annual medical checkup! But I grant you, we don't get so much done these days. Other than the jigsaws, life is not so exciting. Much of our conversation these days revolves around discussion of our last nap and after that we talk about when we might take the next one." He laughed.

"If you think your life is boring you should try staying here." Clive sipped his coffee. "This coffee is nothing like as good as Capuchino Joe's," said Clive.

Albert was getting annoyed. "There you go being negative again. Surely there must be something you're pleased about. I'm not leaving until I get some positivity out of you. What about these two funerals. Did you go to them?"

"You want me to be positive about funerals? Well, I went to the service for one of them which was held here."

"Did you know the deceased?"

"No."

"Then why attend?"

"Something to do."

"How did it go?"

"It was eye-opening. The deceased's name was Gerald. Bit of a skinflint by all accounts." Clive reached into his back pocket, pulled out a folded booklet with a sheet of A4 and began to straighten them out.

"I saved this order of service." Clive then pointed out the A4 sheet to Albert. "I told his daughter I loved her eulogy so much she let me have a copy of it. I knew you were coming over so thought you would like to hear a bit of it."

Albert frowned. "What made you think that?"

Clive ignored him.

"Picture the scene. I enter the solemn Chapel of Rest with the other mourners and sit in my wheelchair at the end of the back row. There's a piece of classical music playing quietly in the background. It sounds vaguely familiar. I look around and the chapel is full of large whiteboards covered in adverts for various products. I cast a curious look at the woman sitting next to me and she tells me Gerald, being the penny pincher he was, did not want to shell out a load of money on his funeral so did it all on the cheap. She says he managed to get enough sponsors that the whole thing was essentially free."

"Free?" queried Albert, "how on earth did he manage that?"

"Well, listen carefully and all will be revealed. At this point I see there is an advert for Hovis. It has a picture of a brown loaf and I then instantly recognise the music. From Hovis's old TV ad! The ad says, Don't say brown, say Hovis. Hovis is the healthy choice, because one day we'll all be brown bread. The lady next to me sees my surprise. She tells me Gerald loved his Hovis. Says he always had a couple of slices for breakfast. She knew because she used to be his housekeeper.

Anyway, then they bring his coffin in. It's made of cardboard! I'd heard about them but it was the first I've seen."

"How sturdy was it?" Asked Albert. "I'd be nervous about falling through it if I was a big guy."

Clive gave him a hard stare. "Hopefully you wouldn't be too nervous, because you'd be dead. But it didn't look that sturdy to me. It was printed with the manufacturer's logo. A line drawing of how to build it plus the company name. 'Folding Early'.

I checked the ads around the room and there were more for DIY coffins in case you were interested. There was one called Natural Endings and another was a website called Comparethecoffin.com.

But let me read this from his daughter's speech.

And so, we are gathered here today to lay to rest Gerald Johnson, a husband, a brother, a grandfather, a friend, my beloved father and yes, a recovering alcoholic. My thanks go out to his fellow AA members who are all here today sitting at the back. He was a great man. An amazing man. But before I get into just how great he was, I would like to say a few words about the financial support to this event from a company that was very dear to my father's heart. And talking about his heart, you all probably know, my father died of a heart attack.

However, he always monitored his health using the latest equipment. Lately this was the wearable Heartthrob 600 device. Whether your heart is grieving or you are monitoring it through regular medical care, the Heartthrob company is there for you. Also, please note there are 10% discount vouchers available for the first six applicants to trial their new Heartthrob 700 device. You can get them from Amazon and any good medical retailers. Sadly, on the day he died, dad was not wearing their patented device. Maybe if he had been ...

At this point she sheds a tear and reaches for a box of tissues. She gestures to her brother. He brings out a fresh box of CleanX and proceeds to move through the mourners offering them to the lachrymose. All the while he has a card around his neck saying 'CleanX are proud sponsors of Gerald's funeral. We dry your tears. We wipe your noses. Soft paper comfort for times of grief and we are cheaper than similar brands!'.

Then, once everyone had dry eyes, her brother says, 'Many of you will know that Gerald did not spend money easily. But there is one thing he would never deny himself and I am certain that many of you here today will have memories of Gerald munching on his favourite snack, Twigitos. Twigitos, the genius snack which combines Twiglets and Doritos. I am sure you all know their slogan '*Crunch time or lunch time, it's always Twigito munch time*. Well, in a special act of kindness, the Twigito company (another sponsor of this event) has kindly provided us all with a unique way of remembering him. If you look under your seats you will each find a pack of Twigitos Cheese and Pickle flavour, Gerald's favourite. Enjoy. Oh, and lawyers for the Twigito company have asked my sister and I to make the following statement.

Will all mourners please ignore any rumours that the Twigito that got stuck in Gerald's throat set off the coughing fit that caused his heart attack. The autopsy results were inconclusive."

"Sounds like a pretty comprehensive eulogy," said Albert. "Did they then go onto actually say something about Gerald?"

"Possibly, but even if they did, none of the mourners could hear much over the rustling of crisp packets and the crunching of Twigitos."

"Wouldn't that spoil their appetites for the food at the reception lunch?" asked Albert.

"Maybe, but most of them thought that knowing Gerald, the Twigitos might be the only free food they were going to get."

"And were they right?"

"Yes."

"So what happened next?"

"I'd had enough of being marketed to by that time so I just sloped off at the same time as the AA group left. I don't think anyone saw me."

"Why did they all leave?"

"Not sure, but the pubs had just opened."

The two men stared out of the window for a while without speaking until Albert broke the silence.

"Funerals always make me think about death. If what you have just told me is the way things are going then it's all very depressing."

"What? Death worries you?" said Clive.

"Your death worries me."

"Well, thank you for being concerned about me but don't worry, I plan to live forever."

"How?"

"I don't know yet but all I can say is hey, so far so good!"

"That's the spirit," said Albert.

The Third Clive Dumper Songbook

Clive's Songs

The Toilet Roll Song

Non panic buyer

You've got sixteen going on seventeen
Toilet rolls, I have none
I'm almost beat, I'm down to one sheet
And soon that will be gone

You have sixteen going on seventeen
Toilet rolls in your hand
Andrex or Tescos, that's how the mess goes
You do not care which brand.

Totally too prepared are you
To face a world of mess
You have so many, I haven't any
You simply couldn't care less

You have sixteen going on seventeen
Loo rolls in every room
You've all the paper, I just have vapour
And that will run out soon

Panic buyer

I have sixteen going on seventeen
Guess what I'm sitting on
My bum is happy, yours will be crappy
The conclusion is foregone

I have sixteen going on seventeen
You haven't really tried
Go help yourself, go clear out a shelf
Happy to be your guide

Totally unprepared are you
And my advice is clear
I'm panic buying, you're hardly trying
While the pandemic draws near

Please no scoffing, now I'm coughing
And I'm in quarantine
I took a six pack then grabbed a twelve pack
Covered in Covid 19

Corona Quarantine

In our house, where we are bored
We have Netflix, praise the Lord
We stay in, don't go for strolls
We all want to guard, our toilet rolls
We check our phones, we sit and Tweet
Social media, is how we meet
We shop online, we drink caffeine
We are waiting for, a new vaccine

We all live in Corona quarantine
Corona quarantine, Corona quarantine
We all live in Corona quarantine
Corona quarantine, Corona quarantine

We wash our hands, clean everything
While we are social, distancing
Let us all begin to sing

We all live in Corona quarantine
Corona quarantine, Corona quarantine
We all live in Corona quarantine
Corona quarantine, Corona quarantine

We wear our masks, don't cough or sneeze
We don't want to cause, anxieties
We may be sick, or in distress
But we want to thank, the NHS

We all live in Corona quarantine
Corona quarantine, Corona quarantine
We all live in Corona quarantine
Corona quarantine, Corona quarantine
We all live in Corona quarantine
Corona quarantine, Corona quarantine
We all live in Corona quarantine
Corona quarantine, Corona quarantine

Albie

What's it all about, Albie?
Is it just for the garbage they bring?
What's it all about - when they chuck it out, Albie?
Are we meant to take all that they give?

Or are we meant to say no?
They say that love is blind, Albie
But you'll end up in some sort of hell
If love also has no sense of smell, Albie

When she chucks you out, Albie
Will it help if you scream and you shout?
Or if you believe - there's a heaven above, Albie
It may help you to recycle love
Then maybe you'll find love again, Albie
Albie

My Favourite Pills

Steroids and statins and other life savers
Could be the cause of my strangest behaviours
Bright coloured tablets to cure all my ills
These are a few of my favourite pills

When the blues strike
When the bills land
When I start to drown
I grab my prescription for favourite pills
Then I don't feel so down

Ketamine, codeine and cocaine and caffeine
Slipped in champagne with a measure of morphine
Then I forget all my fevers and chills
With just a few of these favourite pills

When the blues strike
When the bills land
When I've got no dough
I grab my prescription for favourite pills
Then I don't feel so low

They say Ibuprofen is good medication
Though sometimes a side-effect's bad constipation
But getting things moving is one of my skills
That's when I reach for my favourite pills

When the runs start
When I feel loose
Feel a movement grow
No time to pop any favourite pills
Not when I need to go

There are Bins Comin' in

There are bins comin' in
We love it when we're near 'em
They come from all over the town
They rustle when you hear 'em
And it's our job to clear 'em
Take 'em in, stack 'em up, squash 'em down
There are bins comin' in
There are bins comin' in right now

They deliver us garbage of beauty
In cars that could burst at the seems
To shift it is our bounden duty
Recycling! The job of our dreams.

There are bins comin' in
And each bag someone throws
Can be fragile and easily rip
It may seem to your nose
Someone dirtied their clothes
But we smile, chuck the pile, in a skip
There are bins comin' in
There are bins comin' in right now

They're bringing their bottles and cardboard
Their plastic, their metal, their wood
There's nothing they wouldn't recycle
Their old underwear if they could

There are bins comin' in
The flow never ending
Like a river overflowing its banks
And the crap they are sending
We shall soon be befriending
And for this we must all give our thanks
There are bins comin' in
There are bins comin' in right now

They bring us disposable nappies
Some filled with brown coloured goo
But still, we are all happy chappies
Though sometimes it leaks onto you

So much love comin' in
We should bottle it or can it
From people all over the land
They want to save the planet
But they know that they cannot
So we're here … to give them … all a hand
There are bins comin' in
There are bins comin' in right now

They're bringing us every sad item
Gathering dust in their homes
They bring them in ad infinitum
Every thing every one of them owns

There are bins comin' in
There are bins comin' in right now

A Tip for Us (by Clive the rat)

There's a tip for us
Some trash-filled skip for us
Some place filthy we can infest
Some place … a pest … can rest

There's a dump for us
We could make verminous
There's a home we can fabricate
Find a mate, procreate

Some dump
Somewhere
We'll find a new kind of challenge
We'll find a new way to scavenge
Somewhere

There are dumps for us
With cheesy lumps for us
Rancid and rank rotting food to spare
Much to share, don't despair

There's a dump for us
With dirt and detritus
Some may say that we spread disease
Carry fleas, spread faeces

Some dump
Somewhere
We'll live among their old shoppings
And decorate them with our droppings
Some dump, some tip
Somewhere …

The diets of my mind

Down
Goes my mayo covered sandwich
And the mountain on my plate
Why did thinness go so quickly
Was it something that I ate
When I look into the mirror
I am shocked that I've become
No longer wholly human
I'm half man and half cream bun

Why can't the food I love
Be just as wonderful to taste
Yet not contain the fat
That adds the inches to my waist
Like the sausages I find
In the diets of my mind

There's a tunnel food must follow
It's a tunnel going south
Needing food to fill the hollow
Past my ever-open mouth
Like the chocolate covered doughnut
That's been dipped in double cream
I wake up in the night
To find it wasn't all a dream

I remember in my youth
I was a fit and thinner man
Now my inner bread is buttered
Overspread with inner jam
Just like the sausages I find
In the diets of my mind

All the gravy on the pastry
All the ketchup on the chips
Call to arms a million calories
To march upon the hips
Diners eating in a bistro
Diners in a restaurant
Are all taking second helpings
They can order what they want
And as I look on in envy
Through my salad I can't bear
To eat another cracker
Is like biting on thin air
From the jug of my resistance
The will to diet, though I try
Is spilling out like custard
On some home-baked apple pie

There are tables set before me
Filled with half forbidden food
Tempting never fattening
Swallowed hardly even chewed

I eat food of every kind
Like the sausages I find
All in the diets of my mind

We're the best

We're the best
We're the best
Put our courage to the test
You won't fail to be impressed, you see
We never get depressed
We are great
We can't wait
Facing danger is our fate
As we go to grab a binky
Off a baby not so dinky
We don't stop
We don't rest
We go north, south, east and west
We are fighting for the bullied and oppressed
When we flex our wings
We can do anything
We're the best
We're the best
We're the best

We're the new
Fairy crew
There is nothing we can't do
We even dare to fight a bear
It's crazy but it's true
We care more
Never less
We save damsels in distress
No, we don't know mathematics
But we can do acrobatics
We are cool

We've no fear
It won't take us long to clear
All the evils that infest this fairy world
How is it we can do
The things we have to do
Yes, you guessed
We're the best
We're the best

We're the best
We're the best
And we don't say that in jest
We will challenge any beast you see
And deal with any pest
Don't you say
We are small
Please don't mention that at all
We admit that we are teeny
But we're never ever weeny
We are drab
Not ritzy
Though we may be itsy-bitsy
We can tame a tricksy pixie
And if you ever plan to see
A fairy fantasy
We're the best
We're the best
We're the best

Over the Great Glen

Somewhere over the Great Glen
Fairies fly
We fly down in the dark wood
High in the summer sky

Somewhere inside the Great Glen
Come what may
There's a home where we all live
Work, love and laugh and play

Each day we fly up in the clouds
And look down on the human crowds around us
They spoil our rivers, cut down trees
Build roads and houses as they please
Till they surround us

Somewhere inside the Great Glen
One thing's true
Fairies want to be safe so
Why oh why don't you

If tiny fairy folk like us
Can live our lives without a fuss
Then why oh why can't you

Clive's Poetry

Wandering

I wandered only with a crowd
That drives en masse till Lakeland looms
When all at once I saw a cloud
Of traffic scented exhaust fumes
And trying to park beneath the trees
I ne'er saw queues as long as these

Continuing o'er hill and vale
That wondrous landscape to approve
To insignificance they pale
Compared with trippers on the move
Ten thousand saw I at a glance
Populate that vast expanse

Yet still `tis possible to climb
And lie beside some lonely tarn
To look on waters, stilling time
See distant sheep, low lying farm
And think how peaceful here it gets
Till wak'd by two low flying jets

For oft when from my car I gaze,
In roadside reverie myself to lose
In thinking of how many ways
There be to miss these endless queues
`Tis then I think, `tis good to roam
But better still to stay at home

Clive's Poems for 'Green' Children

Oink oink pink pig
Have you any ham?
No sir, I'm a vegetarian
Fruit for the master
Veg for the dame
And nuts to the little boy who lives down the lane

This little piggy went to market
This little piggy stayed at home
This little piggy had a veggy burger
This little piggy had none
And this little piggy…
Went to the recycle centre on his way home

A sailor went to sea, sea, sea
To see what he could see, see, see
But all that he could see, see, see
Was plastic floating on the sea, sea, sea

Clive's Bad Dog Encounter

Doggy Doo

Well I stepped into some doggy doo
As I walked down the street
I did not know what I had done
But for the people that I'd meet
Those people eager to approach me
Offering their hand at first about to greet me
Then quickly giving a wide berth to me
Or passing out completely

Yes I stepped into some doggy doo
It clung to both my shoes
I did detect an aroma there
But I had not read the clues
And so I walked home more quickly to give distance
To the pong, the pong unknown
But to my surprise the smell, that smell
It followed me back home

I stepped into some doggy doo
It covered up my soles
I don't know what they fed that dog
But it must have eaten several bowls
At last I stood quite still and sought
The source of offence to my nose
And then I sniffed my shoes and said
Never again will I wear those

I stepped out of my doo doo shoes
Got a knife and did my best
To scrape off all that doggy doo
Despite the tightness in my chest
And I determined to scrape and save each scrap
No matter how unpleasant
Placed doo doo in a "doggy bag"
And gift wrapped it like a present

And now I look for doggy doo
As I walk down the street
I want to find that doggy doing
What it does so I can meet
So I can meet the owner of that specimen
Of what they call a man's best friend
And find that owners home address
For there's a gift I wish to send

Clive's Words of Wisdom

When dumping, there are one or two who
Like to use the same loo me and you do
Now some would say this
Was *taking* the piss
But they always *leave* pee-pee …

                                         … or doo-doo."

This toxic tide of things, this septic isle
This mound of muck, this site of scrap
This yearned for Eden, this garden of grime
This den of dust built surely by our sweat
With Health and Safety foremost in our mind
This happy smiling crew, we favoured few
This jewel of junk set in a ring of rubble
Marries our aspirations to our clean air
And divorces our dreams from our despair
Against this endless tempest of trash
This blessed spot, this dump, this tip, this wasteland

Acknowledgements

My utmost gratitude goes to the following: -

>My entire family
>Bob Bray
>Bob Smith
>Margaret Woods
>Dickon Woods
>Jenny Langridge
>Val Skinner
>Paul James

All of these people have provided continuous encouragement, support, thoughts and ideas during the creation of this book of (mainly) nonsense. Therefore, I am not solely responsible for what you may have just read. These people must also share the blame.